ASK ME NO QUESTIONS

ASK ME NO QUESTIONS

MARINA BUDHOS

GINEE SEO BOOKS
ATHENEUM BOOKS FOR YOUNG READERS
NEW YORK   LONDON   TORONTO   SYDNEY

AR4.8
Lex790

Atheneum Books for Young Readers · An imprint of Simon & Schuster Children's Publishing Division · 1230 Avenue of the Americas, New York, New York 10020 · This book is a work of fiction. Any references to historical events, real people, or real locales are used fictitiously. Other names, characters, places, and incidents are products of the author's imagination, and any resemblance to actual events or locales or persons, living or dead, is entirely coincidental. · Copyright © 2006 by Marina Budhos · All rights reserved, including the right of reproduction in whole or in part in any form. · Book design by Sonia Chaghatzbanian · The text for this book is set in Franklin Gothic. · Manufactured in the United States of America ·   10   9   8   7   ·
Library of Congress Cataloging-in-Publication Data · Budhos, Marina Tamar. · Ask me no questions / Marina Budhos.—1st ed. p. cm. · Ginee Seo Books. · Summary: Fourteen-year-old Nadira, her sister, and their parents leave Bangladesh for New York City, but the expiration of their visas and the events of September 11, 2001, bring frustration, sorrow, and terror for the whole family.   ISBN-13: 978-1-4169-0351-2 ·   ISBN-10: 1-4169-0351-8 [1. Illegal aliens—Fiction. 2. Bangladeshi Americans—Fiction. 3. Family life—New York (N.Y.)—Fiction. 4. High schools—Fiction. 5. Schools—Fiction. 6. New York (N.Y.)—Fiction.] I. Title. PZ7.B8827Ask 2006 [Fic]—dc22   2005001831

P-TO 9/08   P.O. 081208

To Alexander Ben Tarun and Raphael Kabir,
the children I see every day

And to those children waiting to be seen

ACKNOWLEDGMENTS

Thanks to my husband, Marc Aronson, ever supportive and ever enthusiastic; the "two grandmothers," Shirley and Lisa, always pitching in; the unflagging Gail Hochman and Joanne Brownstein; the perceptive Ginee Seo for pushing so hard; Naeem Mohaiemen of www.shobak.org, for his invaluable input; and Rita Wolf, for her energy and interest in getting this story out into the world.

ASK ME NO QUESTIONS

ONE

WE DRIVE AS IF IN A DREAM.

Up I-95, past the Triborough Bridge, chunks of black ice floating in the East River. Me and Aisha hunched in the back, a green airline bag wedged between us filled with Ma's *luchis* and spiced potatoes. Abba in the front, clutching the steering wheel, Ma hunched against the rattling door.

We keep driving even as snowflakes clump on the wipers, and poor Abba can barely see. *Coconut flakes,* Ma jokes. *We'll go outside and scoop them up, and I'll make you some* polao. But the jokes lie still in our throats.

Up the East Coast, past all these places I've seen only in maps: Greenwich, New Haven, Providence, Rhode Island. Hour after hour, snow slanting down. And in my head, words keep drumming: *Special Registration. Deportation. Green card. Residency. Asylum.* We live our lives by these words, but I don't understand them. All I know is we're driving straight through to that squiggle of a line on the map, the Canadian border, to apply for asylum.

Unspoken questions also thud in our minds. *What happens if we get stopped and they see Abba's expired license? Should Ma wear slacks and a sweater so she doesn't stand out so much? Should Aisha drive, even though it's supposed to be a secret that she knows how?* We ask some of these questions out loud, and others we signal through our eyes.

When we reach Boston, Aisha wakes up and starts to cry. That's where she hoped she'd live one day. Aisha always knew that she wanted to be a doctor going to Harvard Medical School. Even back in Dhaka she could ace her science and math exams, and when Abba was in Saudi Arabia working as a driver, he used to tape her reports to his windshield and boast about his daughter back home who could outdo all the boys. In those days Abba wasn't afraid, not of anything, not even the men who clucked and said Aisha would be too educated to find a husband, or the friends who worried that he'd be stuck with me, his fat and dreamy second daughter. Sometimes I hate being the one who always has to trail after Aisha. But sometimes it feels safe. I'm nestled in the back, not seen.

Ma pats Aisha on the hand. "Don't worry," she whispers. "All this, it's just for a while. We'll get you in to a university in Canada."

"McGill!" Abba booms from the front seat. "A top-rate school!"

"It's too cold!" I complain.

Aisha kicks me. "Shut up," she hisses, then speaks softly to my father's back. "Whatever you say, Abba."

Aisha and I, we never hit it off, really. She's the quick one, the one with a flashing temper whom Abba treats like a firstborn son, while I'm the slow-wit second-born who just follows along. Sometimes I think Abba is a little afraid of Aisha. It's like she always knew what she wanted, and he was put on this earth to answer her commands. Back in Dhaka when Abba wasn't sure about going to America, she cut out an article and put it in his lap: a story about a Bangladeshi girl who'd graduated top of her class in economics and now worked for the World Bank.

"We may be one of the poorest countries in the world," she told Abba. "But we're the richest in brains."

Abba laughed then. Where did an eight-year-old learn to say such things?

That's the way it always was. Oh, did you hear what the teacher said about Aisha today? "Your sister!" The other girls would whisper to me. "She's different." But what kills me is that Aisha always says the *right* thing. She asks Ma if she's low on mustard oil for cooking, or Abba if he asked the doctor about the better ointment for his joints.

It's hard to have a sister who is perfect.

In Portland, Maine, Abba pulls into a gas station. He

looks terrible: Dark circles bag around his eyes. He's wearing one of his favorite sweater vests, but after ten hours on the road it looks lumpy and pulled. Ma scrambles out of the car to use the bathroom. As she pushes across the station, I notice the pale bottom of her *shalwar kameez* flutter up around her jacket. She presses it down, embarrassed. The attendant is staring at her, the gas pump still in his hand. He's Sikh, with soft, almond shaped eyes, and he smiles at her sweetly, as if he understands, and Ma gets up her nerve and pushes inside the metal door.

After, she takes one look at the two of us and says softly, "We need to stop for some food. These poor girls, they look faint."

When we go inside the small diner, Ma looks funny sitting in the booth, drawing her cardigan across her chest, touching her palms to the ends of her hair. Even though Aisha and I hang out at Dunkin' Donuts and McDonald's all the time, my family rarely goes out to restaurants. Ma's always afraid that they'll ask her something and the English words won't come out right. Now she glances around nervously, as if she expects someone to tap us on the shoulders and tell us to leave. "What if they say no at the border?" she whispers. "What if Canada turns us down?"

Abba sighs, wearily rubbing his eyes. "It could happen. No one guarantees asylum."

We've been over this again and again. We know the risks. If Canada turns us down for asylum, we have to go back across the American border, and Abba will probably be arrested because our visas to America have long since run out. And then we don't know what could happen. Maybe one day we will get U.S. residency. Or maybe we'll just be sent back to Bangladesh. But maybe—just maybe—Canada will let us in.

Abba continues, "Look, Aisha has to begin university in the fall. This is for the best." But he doesn't sound so sure.

Aisha leans her head on Ma's shoulder, her frizzy hair falling in a tumble over her cheeks. "Don't worry, Ma. It'll be okay. We'll get to Toronto and you'll open your restaurant, right?"

A little burn of envy sears right through me. I don't know how Aisha does it, but she always cheers up my parents. Ma and Aisha look a lot alike: They're both fair skinned and thin, and they're these incredible mimics. Ma's always picking things up from TV, where she's learned most of her English.

"Abba, why don't you tell us a story?" Aisha asks.

Abba sits back, his fingers resting lightly on the Formica tabletop, his face relaxed.

I should have asked that. After all, it's usually me who sits around with the elders listening to their stories. Nights when Aisha's in her room studying, I'll sit curled next to Abba and Ma, my head against their legs, and they'll tell me about Bangladesh and our family. Even though we left when I was seven, sometimes if I close my eyes, it's as if I were right there. I remember the *boroi* tree outside our house, the stone wall where Ma slapped the wash dry, the metal cabinet where Abba kept his schoolbooks. Abba carries his stories carefully inside him, like precious glass he cradles next to his heart.

"I'll tell you about the stationery."

We all grin. We've heard this story before, but it's comforting—like sinking into the dense print of one of the old books Abba brought with him from Bangladesh.

"Your great-grandfather used to work as a printer. When he was old and ready to return to our village, the man he worked for gave him a box of the best stationery with his own name printed across the top. Grandfather used to keep that stationery in a special box with a lock. Even when he was old and blind, sometimes he brought it out, and we children would run our fingers over the raised print. Grandfather never wrote anyone with those pages. Who was he going to write to on that fine stationery with the curvy English print?

"After I saw your mother, I wanted to impress her. So I sneaked into my grandfather's room, and I stole a sheet of paper, used my best inkwell and pen, and copied out a beautiful poem. When Grandfather found out, he was furious!"

"Were you punished?" I ask.

Abba nods. "I was, and rightly so. Not only did I deceive my grandfather, but I was not off to a very good start with your mother! She thought I was a rich man who could write poetry. But I was only a poor student who could copy from books." He glances over at Ma. "And I'm still a poor man!"

"Hush," Ma scolds. But I can see she is pleased. She looks gratefully at Aisha, and my stomach twists with jealousy.

"Are you done with those?" I ask, pointing to the last of my sister's fries.

Her nose wrinkles. "No, greedy girl." And she pops the rest into her mouth.

I remember when we first arrived at the airport in New York, how tight my mother's hand felt in mine. How her mouth became stiff when the uniformed man split open the packing tape around our suitcase and plunged his hands into her underwear and saris, making us feel dirty inside. Abba's leg was jiggling a little, which is what it does when he's nervous. Even then we were afraid because we knew we were going to stay past the date on the little blue stamp of the tourist visa in our passports. Everyone does it. You buy a fake social security number for a few hundred dollars and then you can work. A lot of the Bangladeshis here are illegal, they say. Some get lucky and win the Diversity Lottery so they can stay.

Once we got here, Abba worked all kinds of jobs. He sold candied nuts from a cart on the streets of Manhattan. He worked on a construction crew until he smashed his kneecap. He swabbed down lunch counters, mopped a factory floor, bussed dishes in restaurants, delivered hot pizzas in thick silver nylon bags. Then Abba began working as a waiter in a restaurant on

East Sixth Street in Manhattan. Sixth Street is lined with Indian restaurants, each a narrow basement room painted in bright colors and strung with lights with some guy playing sitar in the window. They're run by Bangladeshis, but they serve all the same Indian food, chicken tandoori and *biryani*, what the Americans like. Every night Abba brought home wads of dollars that Ma collected in a silk bag she bought in Chinatown.

The thing is, we've always lived this way—floating, not sure where we belong. In the beginning we lived so that we could pack up any day, fold up all our belongings into the same nylon suitcases. Then, over time, Abba relaxed. We bought things. A fold-out sofa where Ma and Abba could sleep. A TV and a VCR. A table and a rice cooker. Yellow ruffle curtains and clay pots for the chili peppers. A pine bookcase for Aisha's math and chemistry books. Soon it was like we were living in a dream of a home. Year after year we went on, not thinking about Abba's expired passport in the dresser drawer, or how the heat and the phone bills were in a second cousin's name. You forget. You forget you don't really exist here, that this really isn't your home. One day, we said, we'd get the paperwork right. In the meantime we kept going. It happens. All the time.

Even after September 11, we carried on. We heard about how bad it had gotten. Friends of my parents had lost their jobs or couldn't make money, and they were thinking of going back, though, like my father, they'd sold their houses in Bangladesh and had nothing to go back to. We heard about a man who had one side of his face bashed in, and another who was run off the road in his taxi and called bad names. Still people kept coming for *pooris* and *alu gobi* on Sixth Street; still Abba emptied his pockets every night into Ma's silk bag. Abba used to say, "In a bad economy, people want cheap food. Especially cheap food with chili peppers that warms their bellies."

But things got worse. We began to feel as if the air had frozen around us, trapping us between two jagged ice floes. Each bit of news was like a piece of hail flung at us, stinging our skins. *Homeland Security. Patriot Act. Code Orange. Special Registration.* Names, so many names of Muslims called up on the rosters. Abba had a friend who disappeared to a prison cell in New Jersey. We heard of hundreds of deported Iranians from California and others from Brooklyn, Texas, upstate New York. We watched the news of the war and saw ourselves as others saw us: dark, flitting shadows, grenades blooming in our fists. Dangerous.

Then one day my cousin Taslima's American boyfriend came over and explained the new special registration law: Every man over eighteen from certain Muslim countries had to register. Saudi Arabia, Morocco, Pakistan, Bangladesh. Some did, and were thrown in jail or kicked out of the country. More and more we heard about the people fleeing to Canada and applying for asylum there, instead of going into detainment. Abba's friends came over in twos and threes. Ma served them sweets and *doodh-cha*—milky tea—and they'd talk. About starting again in the cold country up north. A new life. The Canadians are friendly, they liked to say.

"There comes a time," Abba said grimly, "when the writing is right there on the wall. Why should we wait for them to kick us out?" He added, "I want to live in a place where I can hold my head up."

One evening Abba came into our bedroom, a quiet, sad look on his face. "Take that down," he said to Aisha. He was pointing to her Britney Spears poster, the only one she was allowed. Ma opened the closets and folded all her saris and *shalwar kameezes* into the nylon suitcases we used when we came here. We could tell no one—not even our best friends at school—what we were doing.

Abba asked me to bring out my map of the northeast. After I laid the map open on the dining table, Abba showed us the thick arteries of highways, the spidery blue line of the border. "There," he said. "We have to go there and apply for asylum."

I swallowed, my throat very dry. What happens if they don't let us in? I kept thinking.

The next morning we woke to a scraping and coughing noise and saw the blue Honda by the curb.

TWO

BY THE TIME WE GET ON THE ROAD AGAIN THE DAY
is in full swing. Tractor trailers are roaring out of the lot,
and there's a pink tinge to the sky. It looks like more
snow though—up ahead, when we turn onto the highway, we can see the gray clouds massed on the horizon.
When Abba cracks open the window, icy wind slices
across my cheek.

We go silent in the car. This is the last stretch, past
the signs for Bass shoe outlets and cigarettes sold
cheap. We're going to leave the main highway soon and
stop at the immigration station on the border between
Vermont and Canada and tell them we're asking for asylum. We'll fill out some forms and it will take a long
time, but then they'll let us go to the other side.

The landscape here is different: clapboard houses
with slanted roofs, church spires, white-columned buildings. I'd always heard about New England. At the college

office in our high school there are lots of catalogues with the kids sitting on lawns in front of buildings like this. When I see those pictures, I want to press myself inside. Just like I want to go to Disney World and Las Vegas and play the slot machines, though Ma would freak. One day I was watching *The Simpsons* and they did this really funny show about Epcot Center. But I can't even laugh at places like that because first I have to go there. Then I can laugh and be sort of above it all. That's how you can tell the immigrant kids from the ones born here. We don't laugh about those places. We just want to go.

The road has turned foggy. The trees sweep past in a wet blur. Abba's driving very slow, hunched over the wheel, trying to peer through the windshield.

We pass a sign: LEAVING THE UNITED STATES OF AMERICA. I see Abba's hand pause as he grabs his chest, rubbing. It hurts, this leaving. We weren't supposed to do this. We were supposed to stay and then one day roll the word in our mouths: *home.* Every inch the car moves forward the word seems to crack, crushed under our tires.

Our car slows and we see four—no, seven—no, maybe a dozen cars ahead of us. Around the bend a Greyhound bus is letting out lots of people: men in long white *kurtas*—knit scarves around their necks—and women whose *shalwar kameezes* stick out from their sweaters. Everyone is stamping their feet in the cold. Just beyond is a low brick building, the red and white Canadian flag snapping on a pole.

A tall man in a brown uniform and hat is moving toward us, waving his gloved hand. Slowly Abba lets down the window.

"Officer, sir?" he asks.

The tip of the man's nose is rosy red, and he's got gingery freckles all over his cheeks. "Passports?" He says it as if he knows not to bother.

"We are applying for asylum in your country, sir," Abba replies. Ma is leaning forward to the left so sharply, I think she's going to fall into Abba's lap.

The man shakes his head, droplets spattering off the brim of his hat. "Sorry. We're full up here. Overwhelmed. People have been coming nonstop, and we can't process them all."

We're still swallowing down the cold, unable to speak. I can see Ma's eyes start to crinkle and turn shiny-wet.

"But sir, we can drive to another post. You just tell me where—"

He shakes his head again. I can see it is a friendly move—he looks sorry to have to say no. "Everywhere. Detroit. All the border crossings. It's been crazy these past few weeks."

No one says a word. I can hear Ma crying very quietly.

From the back Aisha pipes up, "What do you recommend?"

The man takes her in: a seventeen-year-old girl with kohl smudged around her eyes and her frizzy black hair spilling around her parka hood. She's wearing a

Destiny's Child T-shirt and jeans Ma always says are too tight on her.

"The best thing you can do is go back around the American side. I'm afraid they'll probably arrest you if your visa isn't current—" Here he looks at Abba, who is staring dully at the windshield. "My guess is it won't be all of you. I hear they're asking for around five thousand dollars bond. If you put that together, you can come back in a few weeks and try to apply for asylum again."

Abba is squeezing the steering wheel, open-shut, open-shut, just like the massage exercises he did after he got hurt on his construction job. He's hunched over, still as a rock, as if he can't make himself move.

"Sir?"

Still Abba doesn't answer.

"Sir, if you could just turn the car around that way?"

Slowly, Abba puts the car into reverse.

It's funny how long it can take to arrest a person. You'd think it would be like on TV: badges flashing, guns, handcuffs clinked around my dad's wrists. Instead we drive back through the American side, show our passports with the expired visas, and pull around to a low building. We stand on line for hours under fluorescent lights that make my eyes itch, and then, after they look at the papers, they tell Abba to wait. We wait and doze on metal folding chairs, and then they explain everything we already know: Abba will be taken into detention and deportation proceedings might begin. The rest of us can go, and if we come up with the five thousand dollars, Abba will be released and he can apply for asylum on the Canadian side. It could be weeks, though, before they even open our files. Ma digs into her pocketbook and finds numbers of a couple of churches that have shelters that will put us up in Burlington— Taslima, my cousin, found those for her before we left.

Abba, who has taken this all in very quietly, turns to us. He looks first at me, and folds down the collar of my jacket. Then he touches Aisha's hair, once.

"Aisha, Nadira. You are going back."

"Back?" Aisha asks.

He shakes his head. "This is not some kind of quick-quick thing. It could take weeks. And I don't want you children missing school, stranded up here in this cold place. Aisha is about to graduate. She has to finish her year and prepare for college. You want all that to go out the window?"

"How will we get there?"

Abba lets a slow, crooked smile cross his face. "You'll drive."

So Abba knew about her secret driving lessons all along.

"But what about me?" Ma asks.

"You will stay here, at the shelter." He hands her the small silver oval of a cell phone, closes his palm over hers. "You keep this to be in touch with everyone. When the paperwork is done, we'll send for the children."

I feel as if Abba has sliced the air in two, leaving a

ragged gap between them and us. Go back without them? And live where? And how?

Abba lifts the Chinese silk bag out of his coat pocket and hands it to Aisha. "You go stay with Auntie. This is the money for your upkeep. You go to school, you don't say a word to anyone. You do your homework, and you help out in the house. Understand?"

I do understand. That's the way it has always been. Go to school. Never let anyone know. Never.

Aisha is nodding, tears streaming down her face. Abba has cupped a hand around her chin and is speaking softly to her. "You understand I'm doing this for you, nah?"

Still crying, Aisha bobs her head up and down, and I feel that same sharp cut inside. Why is it always Aisha's future?

"Sir?" It's the officer who did all the processing and very quietly explained that Abba would have to go into the detention area until we posted bond. She's holding a thick folder under her arm, and she looks very tired.

Abba stands up, smoothes his palms over his knees. "All right, then," he says in a husky voice. "Time to go."

Now everything happens so fast. I keep thinking that this is a videotape, and any minute now the screen will go blank, and we can rewind and wake up in our apartment and start the day again.

We divvy up the clothes in the suitcases.

"I need a coat," Ma suddenly announces. "If I'm going to stay in this godforsaken place, I need a better coat."

"Ma, where are we going to find you a coat now?" Aisha asks. "We don't even know where the mall is."

"No mall," she replies. "Salvation Army."

Sometimes Ma surprises me. I didn't even know that she knew what the Salvation Army was. But as we were driving into town, Ma's sharp eyes spotted the red-and-white sign of the thrift store. She is already counting her dollars, stretching what she has.

Soon enough we're combing through racks of coats that smell of dust and stale perfume, the pockets stuffed with crumpled tissues and old tickets. I try not to think about Abba in the big concrete room with wooden benches, or about the long, lonely drive ahead. Aisha is holding up coat after coat: a navy blue one with fake white fur trim, a brown tweed with big, deep pockets. Ma doesn't like any of them. "I have to look a certain way," she keeps muttering. "I'm there for your father. I show up in court. I have to look a certain way."

"What way?" we keep asking her, but she just shakes her head, her long braid swinging at her back.

And then she finds it: a purple coat with large, glossy, black buttons and a huge flap of a collar. When Ma puts it on, the coat flares out about her hips like a tent. She swirls around in front of the dirty mirror, laughing. "That's it! I saw a TV show the other day about Jacqueline Kennedy, you remember? Bad things happen to her, and she always looks so nice and trim in public. I always thought if I had to be a white lady, I would want to look like her."

"You and everyone else," Aisha laughs.

But it is good seeing Ma happy for a moment. We find her a pair of galoshes made of milky plastic that she can pull up over her shoes. And the best thing is the whole deal costs us $18.50.

Outside the shelter Ma walks us to the car. She's already put on the coat and I swear it makes her look different—ready to be brave and crisp in front of those immigration authorities. Before we get in she pulls each of us near, presses her cold palms to our cheeks. "You be good," she says.

Aisha has started up the car. As I get into the passenger seat, I see Ma in that purple coat, pressing the black buttons to her chin, those silly galoshes flapping open over her ankles.

Button them up, I want to tell her, but Aisha has swerved the car away.

The sky over Burlington looks like it's made of clear blue glass. I think of Abba behind the cross-wire fence, the way his face broke into wrinkles when he'd heard the news of his detainment. Abba loves this country in his own way; it's like this bowl he carries in his heart— so full, so ready to trust. And right now, as we head to the highway, all I can hear is the sound of his heart shattering.

THREE

EVERY FAMILY HAS A STORY. OURS BEGINS WITH WATER.
My family lived in the part of the world where there
is no difference between land and sea. Bangladesh sits
on the northeast corner of India called Bengal and
looks like a great fan traced with purple-brown veins of
rivers. Once we were part of a kingdom that stretched
from the high mountains of Assam to the dense jungles
of Orissa, sloping down to the sandy beaches of the
holy city of Puri. Then the British, men with ledgers and
rubber boots, arrived and wanted to slice Bengal in
half: one part for the Muslims and the other for the
Hindus. That lasted only a couple of days because a lot
of people protested, and Bengal stayed as one.

Still, no matter where our borders, this is a land
where the earth melts into the sea and back again; where
people sing the same songs and eat the same white
fleshed hilsa fish, wherever they live. There's a Bangla

phrase: *Chor bhanga ar chor gora, ey niye amader jibon.* "Land disappears, land apears—this is our life."

That's why I'm fascinated with maps: They tell one story, yet no matter where people draw the borders, the land tells another. And I like putting the two parts together, figuring out the bigger story.

A long time ago our family lived by the water. We had several small houses arranged in a circle. In one house lived the unmarried sisters who kept their heads covered and bathed in the river every morning and every evening, and sang as the sky turned violet and the land seemed to shift with the turning tide. In another house lived the brothers, and in the big one were the married couples and the elders. The women swept the mud ground with brooms made of twigs and fished in flat bottomed boats. All my great-uncles, I have heard, were great swimmers, diving to the bottom of the marshy river to pull up the jute plants. My great-aunts would split the stalks in the courtyard and then spread them out to dry like the wash.

When the rains came, they fastened all the pots to the roof and tucked their clothes into cubbyholes high in the walls. Sometimes it took an hour just to wade through the swirling brown water to visit a friend in the village. But the rains were good, even when the hurricane winds flung coconuts from the trees; even when the river water rippled so high the tin roofs shuddered and heaved. My family lived in a part of the world where there was no difference between land and sea. The water rose, and you went with it, like the reeds that leaned and bent outside. And after the rainy season was over once more, the land returned. There were no borders. There was only this way of living, back and forth between ground and water, year after year.

But then came the year when the sky did not spill over, and heat flashed across the countryside in a blinding firestorm. Everything shriveled to dirt and dust. My great-grandmother saw the skin on three of her children shrink to dry bone until they died. The sacks of rice were empty—all gone to the British soldiers fighting the Japanese on the Bengal border, or to those who could afford the high prices. It was 1943, a terrible year for our part of the world, and my great-grandparents gathered their pots and pans, their woven rugs, their bits of gold for the daughters' dowries and took their family along the dusty road to Dhaka. There my great-grandfather and grandfather found work in a jute firm.

A few years later the men with ledgers got their way. When the British left as rulers, a new map with new borders was laid upon us. This was called Partition. Bengal was finally lopped in half: one part belonged to the new nation of India and held mostly Hindus. The other part, where we lived, held mostly Muslims and belonged to the other new nation, Pakistan. It was a funny kind of map, since Pakistan lies more than a thousand miles away with India in between. During Partition, there were terrible riots between Hindus and Muslims. Grandmother's childhood friend, Kamla, was chased down the road, her sari a sheet of flames. Half the houses were charred to black ash. And the people from the other side, in what had been West Bengal, kept coming, flooding into our villages the way the water used to come.

These are the stories you hear from your grandmother with the dry rattle in her throat, her teeth stained red from pan and betel leaves; from your abba when he's in a quiet mood and smoothes your hair over and over.

You're only little, but you know it's there: that feeling that you never know what terror will pulse from the ground.

FOUR

YOU'RE ON THE ROAD WITH YOUR SISTER, AND your father is in INS detention, and your ma is sleeping on a shelter cot, and you figure maybe the two of you have a lot to talk about.

We don't.

This registration thing. Going to Canada. Deportation. Aisha hasn't said a word. She doesn't have an answer, the right phrase or sentence to make it all better. Most of the time she drives in angry silence. She won't even let me turn on the radio.

I know things about my family that no one else does. Like about Aisha. I know how hard she works at who she is. Everyone sees her in class, smoothly flipping her hair back from her shoulders before she answers a question. Or sitting on a stage with her hands folded in her lap, chin tipped up, feet tucked beneath her, calmly leading the debate team. Like nothing could shake her up. I know better.

When we first came here, Aisha and me only hung around with Bengali kids, sons and daughters of my parents' friends. Weekends, we'd go over to their places or stay at ours, stuffing our faces with handfuls of *moori* and watching Bollywood movies, dancing along to the songs.

Then Aisha complained that it was no different from being in Bangladesh. She began to study the other kids—especially the American ones. She figured out how they walked, what slang they used. Sometimes she'd stand in front of the mirror practicing phrases like "my mom" or "awesome." The next day she'd come back from school turning the phrase a little differently, shrugging her shoulders in that way that American kids do to show nothing has ruffled them. In sixth grade she figured out which clique of girls she wanted to join. She studied what they wore, their flare-leg pants, their macramé bracelets, and she begged Ma to take her shopping to buy exactly the same things. At first Ma was hurt. Then she figured Aisha's changes might be a good thing if she was going to really make it here.

Aisha can't go to sleep at night unless she lays out the next day's clothes on a chair: her top, her pants, her matching underwear. Then she stacks her notebooks with the spines lined up and zips up her pens and pencils into a plastic bag. After she's crawled under the covers, she keeps talking in the dark, rehearsing who she wants to be the next day.

I embarrass my sister. She won't even go near my

side of the room, where T-shirts and jeans lie crumpled at the foot of my bed along with the little things I collect. My boxes of maps, worn and creased. My bags of Sugar Babies and SweeTarts and licorice scattered and stowed in the drawers. I take after Abba's side of the family, and I'm what they call an average-average kid, pulling in eighty-fives in just about everything. Sometimes the teachers forget me. I sit in the back, and if I'm ever called on, my mind turns murky and slow.

"You go at your own pace," Ma likes to say.

"Yeah, like a turtle without legs," Aisha cracks.

"Shut up!" I cry. Aisha thinks that because she's always zooming ahead she can boss me around. But she doesn't know everything. She misses stuff. Like how sad Ma was when we first came here. Ma would save extra money left over from the food shopping and ask me to buy a phone card so she could call her mother when no one else was home in the apartment; her face brightened the instant she heard the click on the other end. I know how afraid she was in the beginning to go outside. She made Abba install an extra lock on the door and spent hours gazing through the window grates. I know she secretly talked about going back, especially in the winter when the sky turned dark and the cold sliced her ankles and blew up the sleeves of her coat. Once I came home to find the door ajar, eggplant burning in the pan. I ran outside until I found her in the playground, slumped on a bench and crying into a dish towel.

That evening I brought Ma home and put her to bed, smoothing her hair flat with a comb. She stayed in bed for days after. It was only when Abba bought a TV and got cable that her spirits began to lift. She especially loved to watch the cooking shows. She'd stand at the table, spoon held obediently, shouting out new words and phrases. "Stir! Beat! Don't forget to separate!" She often told me, "They're my friends."

Now Aisha and I stop outside Providence at an "all you can eat" buffet in a shopping mall. We push our plastic trays along the metal rollers, staring at the trays of mashed potato and sliced beef in brown gravy and mounds of bright green Jell-O studded with marshmallows. None of it looks very good, but I load up my plate while Aisha takes only salad, bread, and bubbly water.

"This place is disgusting," Aisha whispers to me as we sit down. "Look at those people. They're all overweight and from their skin color you know they've got diabetes and high blood pressure and God knows what else." She pokes at her salad, wrinkling her nose. "Something like one third of Americans suffer from obesity, did you know that?"

Aisha's words sting. My weight is a sore subject in our house. Ma says I'm just a little big for my age. But the clinic doctor says I have to cut back on candy and milk sweets and get more exercise. Nobody else in our family is fat, and sometimes I feel like I've been beamed in from another genetic planet. I took an extra period of gym, though most of the time the black girls pushed me around and laughed me off the basketball court. I'm not good at any of that stuff. I'm kind of clumsy, and I get too winded when I run.

Aisha always looks at me as if there's something lazy in me that makes me eat all that bad food. As if I let the bad parts of America get into my bloodstream like some high-cholesterol poison, fattening me until I'm stupid. "You know," she says. "Now that I'm in charge of you, I think it's time you went on a diet. If we're going to move to Canada, it's a good time to make a fresh start."

"Who says you're in charge?" I jab some french fries in my mouth. They're soft and greasy and leave a gassy bubble under my ribs.

Aisha's eyes narrow. "I'm older."

"So?"

"I'm the one who can drive."

"You're not supposed to," I tell her. "Uncle says girls aren't allowed."

She throws back her head and laughs. "Oh, Nadira. Don't be stupid. Abba and Ma are completely enlightened. Do you think they would have let me drive the car and take you back if they believed all that gender crap?"

A soft heat pulses behind my eyes, making them sting. I hate it when Aisha uses words like "gender" and "enlightened." She and Taslima talk a lot like that. They'll huddle in a corner at family gatherings and shoot out their quick scornful sounds, cutting up everything, as if they know better. They don't do it so much in front of the grown-ups because even though she talks big, Aisha's also respectful of elders. That's the way we were raised.

"When we get back, Uncle and Auntie will be in charge of us anyway," I tell her. "They'll call the shots."

"Oh, Nadira." She says my name quietly as if she really is sorry. "It's just us now. Uncle and Auntie can only do so much. We're not in Canada, we're not in America, we're not in Bangladesh. We're on our own."

"So?"

"So we have to stick together. Not fight."

She holds out her hand as a peace offering. I look at her slender wrist, her single bangle glinting against the bone. No way am I sticking together with Aisha. What that really means is I'm supposed to do whatever she says, and then she gets all the credit. "Forget it," I reply, and then I shove a spoonful of Jell-O in my mouth, get up, and head to the buffet for more.

FIVE

TUESDAY MORNING AISHA AND I ARE BACK AT
Flushing High as if nothing happened.

We're not the only illegals at our school. We're everywhere. You just have to look. A lot of the kids here were
born elsewhere—Korea, China, India, the Dominican
Republic. You can't tell which ones aren't legal. We try
to get lost in the landscape of backpacks and book
reports. To find us you have to pick up the signals. It
might be in class when a teacher asks a personal question, and a kid gets this funny, pinched look in his eyes.
Or some girl doesn't want to give her address to the
counselor. We all agree not to notice.

I remember when I was little, crouching in a corner of
the playground and hearing a group of girls chant: *Ask
me no questions. Tell me no lies.* That's the policy at
school. *Ask me no questions*, we say silently. And the
teachers don't. "We're not the INS," I once heard one

of them say. "We're here to teach." But sometimes I feel like shaking their sleeves and blurting out, *Ask me. Please.*

This morning Aisha and I are standing by the lockers on the first floor when Mr. Friedlander, the college counselor, comes hurrying up to us. He looks happy—really happy.

"Aisha!" he calls. "I was looking for you yesterday." His brow wrinkles a little. "Were you sick?"

Aisha tosses her hair back from her shoulders and gives him a sweet smile. "Nothing big. Just a little stomach flu."

A flicker of tension twitches between us: Five times on the way to school Aisha told me not to say anything about our trip to the border, not even to Lily Yee, my best friend at school.

"I've been on the phone with Mrs. Jones at the Barnard admissions office."

Aisha stiffens a little, her elbows drawn back at her sides. "That's great."

"They're very interested in your application. So I've scheduled an interview."

"Wow." The two of us stare for a few seconds at Mr. Friedlander. He dresses a little funny, in sky blue shirts with bow ties and tweed jackets, and he's always rattling off facts that have nothing to do with math, the subject he teaches. He once lectured Aisha and me about the ancient city of Harappa. All the kids say he's one of the coolest teachers in school since he gets to know everyone really well. Poor Mr. Friedlander doesn't have a family. So sad, Abba says. But he doesn't seem sad to me.

Mr. Friedlander is the coach for the math team, and Aisha's one of the stars—she can do sums and equations so quick, people think she cheats with a calculator. Ever since he had Aisha in geometry and heard that she wanted to go to Harvard and be a doctor, Mr. Friedlander has made Aisha his little project, recommending her to Mrs. Rosen for the debate team, too. Because Aisha's such a good mimic, she's a great debater—she can actually imagine what other people are thinking, say it better than they do, and then turn the argument her way. "You will be a lawyer one day, not a doctor," Abba likes to joke.

Mr. Friedlander, Mrs. Rosen, none of them know that we're illegal. After Aisha filled out the college applications, we kept hoping our immigration papers would go through so everything would be aboveboard. She wrote in the space for immigration status "visa pending." When Mr. Friedlander pressed Aisha about finishing the financial aid forms, Aisha lied. She said that the family had saved up a lot of money and that all the relatives were planning on chipping in and helping to pay for her education.

Now Mr. Friedlander puts his hands on his hips and smiles. "So we're set, then?"

Aisha nods.

"Great. I'll call you tonight when I know what day and time."

Aisha freezes, her hand on the locker door. Of course he can't call: We don't live at home anymore. The only thing left is a wilted chili plant on the kitchen windowsill and a FOR RENT card stuck in the front window. "Do you think you could just send a note to me later?" she asks. "Our phone—it's broken, and the phone company isn't sure when they'll fix it."

"Sure. I'll do that." He does an odd squint, and then he looks at me, grinning. "So, Nadira, not bad for your big sister, eh?"

"It's great," I reply.

"In a couple of years," he says, wagging his finger, "we're going to start on you."

After school I go to visit my Ali-Uncle at the magazine shop. Ali-Uncle is not my real uncle; we just call him that, like we do for all my parents' male friends. He's not as old, either, as all the other uncles, but he likes to wear a long *kurta* and he has a beard and he prays five times a day. Abba and Ma, they do some of the holidays, like they fast for Ramadan, but it's been a long time since I've seen Abba pull out the prayer rug from the closet. Ali lives by himself in a room over a dry cleaner's. In the mornings he works at a discount electronics store, moving boxes in the stockroom. Afternoons, he comes here to watch the register, and then stack the newspapers and shut down the place. When it's time for him to roll out his little rug in the back alley and do his evening prayers, I stand at the cash register and help gather the last papers.

The rest of the time he's always at the mosque a few blocks away, where he sits cross-legged on the small carpets and explains the Koran to the little boys gathered around him, or he recites poems by Tagore or Nazrul, the most famous Bengali poets. Ma says Ali-Uncle is like a guardian spirit. He watches over others and makes sure we are safe from harm.

I'm turning the corner when behind me I hear the *thump-thump* rumble of a car stereo, and Tareq comes squealing to the curb. Tareq drives a souped-up car with tinted windows and a major sound system. "Low-life," Aisha calls him. That's because he dropped out of school. He's always got an angle—he worked on construction crews for a while, drove for a car service, and then got into some deal at a gas station where he pretended to man the pumps but in the back unloaded crates of radios and CD players.

Ma calls him *Bagh'a*, which means "tiger" in Bangla, because he's got this wide face with narrow eyes and a fearsome temper. Tareq wears his baggy jeans just so—flopped over his tan Timberland work boots ("And what kind of work is that boy doing so he wears expensive boots like that?" my mother always scolds), a black comb hiking out of the back pocket. For a while there were rumors that he was in a gang that was always busting up parties at the *bhangra*-music clubs.

"Nadira!" he shouts to me now.

He's sitting in the driver's seat, one hand loose on the wheel. "Hear your dad's in some trouble."

"No trouble," I reply.

"Not what I was told."

Half the time I don't know what to make of Tareq—he makes me mad and anxious, but he's also so strong and sure of himself. The lock pops up, and Tareq waves me into the car. I climb into the passenger seat, my nylon backpack squashed down by my feet.

"Your dad wants, I can take care of it."

"What do you mean?"

"There's places you can buy what you need." He taps his steering wheel. "You think everyone gets a green card playing by the rules?"

He presses the button on the glove compartment, extracts a pen and a scrap of paper, scribbling some numbers down. "That's my cell," he goes on. "Call me any time."

I stuff the paper into my pocket.

"Nadira!"

Ali-Uncle is standing outside the magazine shop, hands on his hips. I give Tareq a sheepish look and climb out.

I brace myself for a lecture from Ali-Uncle about Tareq, but it doesn't come.

Instead he says with a smile, "You came back safe." Behind me I hear the squeal of tires, and Tareq's car is gone, throbbing in the distance.

"Can I have a Coke?" I ask.

He smiles and scribbles an imaginary pad with his finger. "I'm keeping a book for how many you've drunk, Nadira."

The shop is like a long closet, and the two of us can barely stand next to each other without one of us bumping into the magazine stand or the cash register. Now I wish it were bigger, because Ali-Uncle keeps looking at me with his soft, worried eyes. The first night after we returned, Auntie had called our friends, cupping her palm over the receiver and telling everyone what had happened to us when we tried to go to Canada.

"You mustn't fret about your father. He'll be all right. He's such a strong man. And your mother, she'll make sure he gets his papers right."

We work silently together, cutting off the top of the first page of the newspapers and putting them in stacks, though the whole time I can feel Ali-Uncle's eyes on me. "Not to worry, not to worry," he mutters several times under his breath. By the time we're done, I'm so jumpy and tired I don't even want the bag of Sugar Babies he tosses in my direction.

"Nadira." We're standing outside the store, the grate pulled down and the lock attached. Dirty slush gurgles into the street drain, and a damp, chilly wind seeps down my collar. I look up at the black sky, and I wonder if it's dark in Vermont, too. How does Ma make her way back to the shelter when it's time to go to sleep?

Ali-Uncle is speaking, so I pull my thoughts from Ma and try to pay attention.

"In this country we are still only visitors. We must be very careful. If we offend or break the law, we may bring the wrath from our hosts." He sighs. "Boys like Tareq, they don't think. They just do. They're not good for our community. They're vultures feeding off of our fears."

I squirm away, not wanting to hear his lecture.

"There's something else," he continues. "If by chance one day I too have to go away . . ." He gestures toward the street where white points of headlights stab past. "You must say nothing. Not to your parents, not to anyone." I must look alarmed because he adds quickly, "There's nothing wrong. It's just . . . there may come a time when I have no place to stay. You understand?"

I do. I hear these stories all the time, especially these days. Friends of my parents who decide to move to a different apartment, another state, hoping the authorities won't track them down. But I don't like the way Ali-Uncle is looking at me, his bristly eyebrows bunched together. I don't like the way the adults have been talking to me since this all began. Either they speak like I'm a little baby who can't understand the stupidest thing, or they gaze at me with the weight and sadness of the world behind their eyes, making me feel so confused I wish they'd just shut up. Now I feel even worse because it's happened to Ali-Uncle, who was always so calm and reassuring. He's already turned away and started walking down the block. He holds his collar tight against his throat. The bottom of his *kurta* blows against his knees like two flimsy pieces of wash, and the words inside me are stones in my mouth.

Back at the apartment I find Auntie on the phone with Ma. Auntie's dressed in an old cotton robe, fuzzy slippers flapping at her heels, her curls held flat with rows of shiny black bobby pins. Auntie's the opposite of Ma: She's soft and round faced, like Abba, and is always clucking over who has what DVD or TV set and where she can buy percale sheets at a discount. She even went and got herself a part-time cashier's job at a ninety-nine cent store, which made Uncle furious. "I didn't come to this country so my wife could work!" he complained, but Auntie paid him no mind, buying herself a brand-new rice cooker and leaving his supper on the stove so she could go off to work.

Today Auntie's excited, and she keeps shouting into the mouthpiece as she paces back and forth. It only takes her five steps before she's reached the end of the living room and bumped into our suitcases. For now Aisha and I are sleeping in the living room on the fold-out sofa, and Taslima is in her tiny bedroom. It's really a corner of the same room, but Uncle built two walls and a door, giving her enough space for a bed and a desk.

"That's good!" Auntie keeps saying. "Good! Tomorrow, then!"

When she sees me, she hands me the receiver. "Talk to your mother."

"How are you, Nadira? Holding up?" my mother asks.

"Yeah."

"You heard? With our savings and the money Auntie and Uncle have wired, I have enough for the bond now, so tomorrow I go to fetch your father."

"How's he doing?"

"As well as can be expected," she says in English. Where did she get that one from? I think. Ma went to convent school for a few years until her family couldn't pay, and she sometimes turns out phrases like that; they sound like the high, pretty trill of a bird, perfect and light. "Your father says he's thinking that the first thing he needs to do is learn how to follow Canadian hockey." She laughs. "And you and Aisha?"

"She's okay. She's got some Barnard interview or something."

"That's wonderful!"

"Yeah." I don't know what else to say. Whenever we talk about Aisha I feel two things: I'm proud, like I get to rest for a minute in the glow of being her baby sister, but then I get mad and wish there were some way I could make them notice me too.

"Nadira, I want to talk to you. I'm glad Aisha's not there for the moment." Ma's voice lowers a little, and a stiffness settles under my ribs. There it is again: the adults getting that funny sound in their voices. "You know Aisha, with that temper of hers. She and Taslima, the way they can go off."

"Yes, Ma."

"You're such a good girl. So sweet and patient. I

thank God he gave me a daughter as patient as you. You keep an eye on them."

That's not all I am, I want to say, but she has already hung up.

I head for the kitchen to eat some of my aunt's fish fry. Then I try and do my homework at the dining room table. It's hard. Auntie is so noisy in the kitchen, and when Taslima comes in, they start to quarrel.

Taslima's not American born, but it's almost like she is. She goes to Queens College, and Ma's always clucking over the way Taslima dresses in low-low hip-hugger jeans and tight black T-shirts. When she was in high school, she used to sneak out of her bedroom window and climb down the fire escape to hang out with her friends. Recently she cut her hair short, so it sticks up from her scalp in bristly spikes. Worst of all she's been spending time with some kind of *shada-chele*—a white guy. A few weeks ago she had the nerve to come over to our house with her *shada*. His name is Tim, and he has hair the color of orange wheat and freckles on the backs of his hands. He's so tall he had to stoop a little when he shook Abba's hand.

Turns out Tim is a law student, and he works for a human rights organization. That's how he and Taslima met—she plans on going into law too and he was her supervisor when she did an internship.

"It's crazy," Uncle muttered when Tim came over to explain the Special Registration law. "We fought a war to get free of Pakistan, and now they put us in with them."

Taslima made a face. "You think they know the difference? Please. All brown people are the same to them."

Abba looked at her sternly. "And please, young lady. We don't talk that way in this house. This country has been good to me. It is I who am breaking the law."

For days after Tim's visit everyone quarreled. Abba wanted to register—it had gone on too long, this hiding without papers. "Are you mad?" Uncle cried. "You register and you only make trouble for yourself! Who will know the difference if you don't register? You can just keep going, earning your dollar." Uncle thought it was best to lie low, wait it out, or go back to Bangladesh. "Back!" Taslima yelled. "You expect me to go back, and I'm not even done with university!" Uncle, who was always angry at Taslima for being so disobedient, shot back, "And how do you expect me to pay those fees if I cannot even support my family here?"

Now Auntie scolds her for coming in so late. She still doesn't like her going with that Tim boy, even if he is good-hearted and is helping us. "I never said you were permitted to date," she says, and Taslima slams into the bathroom, and soon Auntie's pounding on the door.

I press my hands to my ears and try to concentrate on my geometry homework. The figures jerk like dangling sticks on the page. I wish I could be like Aisha and just focus. Or Taslima, talking back. But that's not me. I like staying quiet and still, taking in the words of the grown-ups. Only sometimes it feels lonely being this way, as if their voices are turning me to heavy stone. Sometimes I wish I could lift out of myself and do something that really counts.

SIX

WHEN I WAKE THE NEXT MORNING, THE SNOW HAS melted and is dripping in a noisy patter off the fire escape. The window over the sofa is open a crack, and the air blows in, sweet and warm. I dig down deep into the suitcase and pull out a T-shirt and jeans and my nylon spring jacket. I can imagine Ma standing in the doorway, sighing, Why do you have to dress like a boy?

Uncle is sitting at the dining room table running a stiff bristle brush over his black shoes, the ones he uses for his catering job. I remember two years ago when he first got the job: He proudly brought home a new pair of black pants with satin ribbons running down the legs and a crisp white shirt zipped in a plastic bag. The money was good in the beginning—a thousand a week, which is why Taslima could go to college and they could buy this big sofa instead of sitting on the floor with pillows and rugs. Then Uncle's supervisor started to call less. Now days can go by before Uncle gets another call. Still every morning he brushes and polishes his shoes and makes sure his black pants and shirt are ready. Still he sits by the phone, waiting.

Uncle is tall and his nose is a funny curved beak, making him look cross-eyed. He doesn't talk too much either; his words are sour balls in his mouth. I know he wasn't too happy about us coming over to America. "You don't have a good job, it's not so easy," he kept telling my mother. "That husband of yours, he's a dreamer, and one day his dreams are going to get him in trouble."

He's always finding fault with Abba, especially when Abba lavishes presents on Ma and buys her all kinds of gadgets for the kitchen: vegetable scrubbers, garlic peelers, fancy knives. "You better watch out," he warns. "You spoil your wife too much." And then there's his annoyance with Taslima and Aisha. Uncle says he's not sure who's worse—Taslima with her big mouth or Aisha with the crazy stars in her eyes—but he doesn't like the way they're always egging each other on. "This house is being run by women," he grumbles in that sour-mouth way of his. "Daughters are not daughters, and wives don't act like wives."

"You ready to go live in Canada?" he asks me when I join him at the table.

I shrug.

"It's cold there. Not going to be so easy. Not as many Bangladeshis as here."

"Abba says that doesn't matter. That the most important thing is we get to go to school and we're legal and—"

"Legal!" He slaps his brush down on the newspaper. "You think just because you're legal everything's a sunny day all of a sudden? When I get my residency, will the man on the street look at me any different? Will I get a better job?" He leans over and stares at me, hard. "Look around you, Nadira. What do you see? Everyone is going home. Your Ali-Uncle, he told me he knows of four men who have disappeared. Four!"

I think about what Ali-Uncle said to me yesterday evening as we stood on the cold street corner, and I shiver. "But, Uncle, Abba says that this is just a bad time, but we can always go across the border and start again."

Uncle grabs me by the arm, pushing his face close to mine. I've never seen him like this: eyes black and wild-looking, nostrils flared.

"Borders!" he yells. "What do you know of borders! Do you know what happened to my grandmother when she fled West Bengal? They murdered her! Neighbors turned assassins! Those Hindu mobs, they came upon her in the road, and they killed her. And not just her, but two of her children! Little boys, younger than you! What about that? You think you can just start again? I see you there! Sitting around, fat and lazy! What are you going to do?"

"Please, Uncle—"

"I tell you what we have to do. We have to stop asking Allah for so much. Because everything we ask for on this earth, every home we beg for, it is always taken from us."

"Ahmed!" Auntie is standing in the bedroom doorway, a comb in one hand.

Uncle drops his hands as if suddenly remembering himself. He lifts himself up from his seat. "I'm giving this girl a little lesson. That father of hers is filling her head with all sorts of nonsense."

"Lesson, ha. You're just a bitter man trying to poison this young girl. No wonder Taslima has that sharp tongue of hers. She's trying to cut out all the rot."

I draw my breath in, stunned. I've heard Auntie and Uncle quarrel before, but never like this. Slowly lowering his hand, Uncle leaves the room. There's a red mark on my arm from where he grabbed me, and I'm suddenly afraid.

As Auntie makes me breakfast, she tells me Uncle's upset because a friend from work was picked up by the INS and thrown in jail, and his wife came to see Uncle, begging for help. He's been hearing lots of bad stories, and it's filling him up like a sharp pickle. Uncle stews in all those nasty words, and he can't help himself—his feelings ooze out of him until he's short-tempered and picks a fight over the smallest of things.

"There are two kinds of people in the world, Nadira," Auntie tells me. "Those that hear bad news and want to run away and those that dig their feet in and want to fight." She laughs. "Taslima, she was put on this earth to be a thorn in her father's side. Because she will always fight. Fight, fight, fight, even when it's time to run."

The whole way to school I keep thinking about what Auntie said about Uncle and Taslima. Ma has always told me that Uncle has a sour nature because he's borne too many losses. There was Partition, when half his family was killed, and then his twin sons who died of a fever back in Dhaka. And then there's Taslima, who's done all kinds of crazy things. One time she came home with two silver studs in her ear; another time she called Auntie up and said she and some friends had driven upstate to some college, and they were spending the weekend there. Nobody we know would ever do such a thing, much less talk to their parents that way. But that's Taslima—it's like she's got this ring of angry flames around her, daring you to touch her and be burned.

As I get on the bus to school, Uncle's words keep hammering at me. *What about you, Nadira? Fat and lazy? What will you do?*

How do I fight? I think. What can I do?

"Where you been?"

I turn. Lily Yee is clutching the overhead bar. Lily is plump, like me, with straight black hair cut into a ragged bowl cut.

I shrug. "Around."

"I was looking for you at Dunkin' Donuts." She grimaces. "My dad went away for a whole day and came back at four in the morning. My mother went crazy and threw a lamp at him."

"Wow," I say, though not very enthusiastically. I don't have the energy to listen to Lily right now.

Usually when I'm not working with Ali-Uncle in the afternoon, Lily and I like to sit at the Formica tables and eat jelly doughnuts and talk. Sometimes about school, or about our families. She's the only one I can tell things to, but today there's a tightness in my chest because I can't say what's going on.

Lily has her own secrets. Once she saw her father kissing another woman in a restaurant. Her parents own a few businesses: two dry cleaning stores and a nail salon. Lily thinks the woman was one of the manicurists—she once pointed her out to me—though she isn't sure. At night she can hear her parents arguing. Often she shows up at one of the dry cleaning stores to help, and her father is out. He comes back, patting the pockets of his coat, saying he had some problems with an employee. She doesn't know what to think. Lily worships her father. He came to America and did everything for her and her brothers and her mother, buying a nice house where Lily has her own room and an iPod. Her mother, she says, is mean as can be, and sometimes locks her father out or makes him sleep on the downstairs sofa.

As we're getting off the bus, she asks me, "What should I do? I can't ask him because he'll say I'm being disrespectful."

Most of the time I can listen to Lily go on about her family. Now her complaining makes me hurt, like I'm still pressed against the wall with Uncle's sour breath warm on my face.

"I don't know, Lily."

"Can you meet me after school?"

"I'm not sure."

"What is with you?"

Inside math class, I slump in the back across from Lily. Usually I like geometry. I don't pull ninety-eights and hundreds like Aisha, but Mr. Chin tells me I have a knack for visualization, and he sometimes gives me three-dimensional problems for extra homework. "Computers," he advises me. "Tell your parents that's what you should do."

Today he's walking up and down the aisles, handing out quizzes. He snaps one down on my desk and smiles. "This should be nothing for you, Nadira."

I try to focus on the numbers, but they keep jumping off the paper. I look over at Lily, who is busy writing away. I try a few of the problems, then stop. Lily is hunched over her seat, scratching her answers. I shoot my hand up.

"Yes, Nadira?"

"Bathroom pass."

"Can't it wait?" Mr. Chin glances at the clock. Sighing, he hands me the flat wooden pass and tells me to hurry up.

The bathroom stinks of Clorox, and wads of tissue

are jammed in the toilets. I turn the water on full blast at the sink and scrape my face with the rough brown paper towels. In the mirror all I see is a fat girl with chubby hands. I look stupid, not like someone who's good at math or anything else. And definitely not like a daughter who can help her parents. Behind me the door opens and some girls, probably seniors, come sauntering in; their loud voices bounce off the tile walls.

An elbow digs into my side. "Ooh, ooh." I swerve around, arms flailing. "Don't fall over, big girl. You don't want to crush us!"

Suddenly the door swings open again, and the hall monitor is rattling her keys. "Ladies! You want to break up the tea party?"

Quickly I angle my way out and hurry back to class. Back to the test I can't seem to take. Walking down the aisle, I try to peer at Lily's answers, but her hand is slanted across the page.

Just as I'm sliding into my seat, I feel a cold hand on the nape of my neck. It's Mr. Chin. My heart starts up, fast and crazy.

"I hope I didn't just see what I thought I saw, Hossain."

Lily thinks Mr. Chin's just a big joke—a failed engineer with chalk on his fingers and body odor. But I know that when he uses my last name, I'm in trouble.

"What's that, Mr. Chin?" I ask. My voice is a tight, squeaky thread.

He lets his hand drop. "Just finish up."

I try to still the wild pounding in my chest. By the time the bell rings, I've managed to finish only twelve of the twenty questions.

At lunchtime Aisha comes up to me in the cafeteria. It's rare Aisha and I hang out in school; she's got her friends, who sit together at a table at the far end. The perfect girls, I call them. Rose Chu; Kavita Menon; and Risa Sharansky, who probably one day is going to be famous because she's this really great violinist. They flip their hair back and huddle together, and there's always some teacher hovering in their orbit, touching their shoulders with just the tips of her fingers as if they're made of pretty glass.

"Hey." Aisha's holding her tray of juice and a plate with slices of turkey and gravy. She nods to their table, inviting me to join them.

"So what colleges did you finally wind up applying for?" Risa asks Aisha as we sit. "My mom made me narrow it down to seven. She said there was no reason to put down so many safety schools."

When we sat down at the dining room table and went through stacks of college applications for Aisha a couple of months ago, our status still wasn't cleared up. The applications cost so much money—hundreds and hundreds—but Abba said, "No matter." Aisha filled them out herself, writing on the lines in her neat, boxy handwriting.

Now Aisha blushes to the roots of her hair. "I did a

lot of them. Actually I was thinking about . . . McGill."

Risa looks puzzled. "McGill? In Canada? Why all the way up there? It's in another country."

Aisha shrugs. "You never know. My dad, he may get a job there. And we've got some cousins near Toronto, in Scarborough." She's lying, but I can feel how humiliated she is. All those fat envelopes sent off, and now nothing. Only this feeling of windy space beneath our feet, like the humming road coming back from the border; the jittery sense that nothing is right. Risa, Rose, Kavita—they're legal, for years and years. They're the perfect candidates, the ones you read about in the paper: Little Miss Westinghouse or Miss *New York Times* Scholarship. There's a testy competition among the four of them, even though they're all friends.

After the others get up to clear their trays, Aisha says to me, "Listen. I heard some really amazing news today."

"Yeah?" My heart gives a little lift. Maybe she's heard something about Abba.

"I've been nominated."

"For what?"

She pauses. "For valedictorian." She smiles. "Remember I told you a few weeks ago that Friedlander had put in his vote for me? And Mrs. Rosen too?"

"What a surprise," I remark. "The Aisha Fan Club."

She scowls. "Why not? What do you think I've been working for all these years?"

Before I can help myself, I've jumped up from the

table and shoved Aisha's tray back at her so the gravy goes slopping onto her neat buttoned blouse. "What are you talking about, Aisha?" I whisper hotly. "You and your little perfect scores and your perfect this and that? Who cares if you're valedictorian? You're not going to college! You're not going anywhere!"

Aisha looks as if I've socked her in the chest. She sits back, breathing hard. Her frizzy hair has straggled loose from her braid. She blinks away a few tears. The others stare at me in shock. Then she picks up her tray, stiffly, and walks down the aisle of tables. I'm left staring at my own tray. Strange, nasty thoughts swarm into my head. I've never made my sister cry before. It seems impossible. Aisha is too strong, too smart for me. But this is different. It's like having a new kind of power, black and ugly, like what Uncle did to me this morning.

And the weird thing is: I like it.

When we get home from school that day, Auntie and Tim are sitting on the couch. Auntie's in a rumpled *shalwar kameez*, and hair has straggled loose from her bun showing streaks of gray.

"What's the matter?"

Tim stands up, shakes out his jeans around the knees. He suddenly looks awkward and gangly; his arms and legs are too big for the rest of him. "Aisha. Nadira. We had a little bit of a setback today. Your father's bond was denied. It seems—"

"If you want to know," Taslima adds in, "those bastards have decided to hold him. They say he needs to be questioned."

"Questioned?"

"They say he lied on his application. About where he lived. Not reporting when you guys moved."

"But Mr. Rashid was supposed to straighten all that out—"

"Apparently he didn't."

"And they're looking at some political affiliation."

Aisha and I look at each other, puzzled. "Affiliation?"

"It's nothing. You know he hasn't done anything. But there's some money he gave to the mosque. He signed his name and everything. And now they're investigating everyone in the mosque."

My head spins. None of this makes any sense. Abba political? At most he likes to sit around with his friends and talk about the World Cup.

Auntie slaps her hands on her lap. "I told him never to sign anything! Never!"

"So what does this mean?" Aisha asks.

Tim shrugs. "There are lawyers keeping track of the situation now. But they can detain him for as long as they like if they think he's violated his visa—even in the smallest way. Or if there's a political affiliation that's suspect. And as for your asylum application—"

"That's finished," Aisha says dully.

"You just have to wait and see what happens here."

I just sit there on the couch feeling as if it's all my

fault. Ever since I woke up and Uncle said those bad things and then later at school I tried to cheat on my test and said even worse things to Aisha—it's like we brought it on ourselves, all this misfortune, like dark cold water pulling us down.

Aisha says nothing. Her slim body seems to take it in, bit by bit, until she's shivering just a little. I notice the gravy stain on her shirt. The ragged edges of it are brown. Aisha picks up her book bag and turns toward Taslima's bedroom.

"Aisha?" Auntie calls after her.

There's no answer on the other side of the door.

"Nadira, go to your sister. Please," Auntie begs.

But I can't, I think, hunching in my chair. I can't go to my sister. I can't go to anyone, not now.

SEVEN

THEY ALWAYS SAY THAT NO MATTER WHAT HAPPENS to Bangladeshis—floods, storms, droughts, riots, strikes—we keep going. Generation after generation the water and the land melt and blur; people move across borders that make no sense. We cram into our land, which is no bigger than Wisconsin. We know how to save our money and work. We take our baths every morning and evening, no matter what. We just keep going and try to do the right thing.

When Abba and Ma were growing up, the land began to rumble and shift again. The people wanted to shake loose the new borders; they no longer wanted to be joined to that other Pakistan a thousand miles away. Soldiers roamed the streets speaking their strange, dry language, beating students with the hard butts of their rifles. Abba had an older brother, Naseem, who used to meet in secret and speak the forbidden words of

Tagore, whose poetry was banned. Abba loved Naseem: Though a full ten years lay between them, Naseem thought nothing of letting Abba tag along when he went to his meetings, or when he smoked rolled up cigarettes on the sly with his friends.

And then one day Naseem disappeared, gone to join the *Mukti Bahini*, "Freedom Fighters," who wanted their own nation. Every day my grandmother pressed her forehead against the window grate, praying her eldest son would walk down the dusty street. But it was not to be. The more Grandmother prayed, the worse the news became. They heard about university students shot and professors murdered on their pillows. They heard about Freedom Fighters mowed down in dirt pits, Hindu villages riddled with gunshot. Millions of refugees formed an endless, tattered stream trudging toward Calcutta, in India. And when the fighting was over, when the soldiers fled in their rattling Jeeps, my grandmother learned that Naseem-Uncle was buried in a field of flowering mustard plants.

Abba never forgot Naseem-Uncle. During the years he was growing up and studying for his engineering degree, he never forgot the songs Naseem used to sing to him late at night. And one warm evening Abba went to a *mela*—a fair—for the *Pohela Boishakh*, or Bengali New Year. He sat on the grass and listened all evening long as people stood on the stage and recited and sang songs.

It was then he saw Ma sitting not far away with her sisters. He saw how she dipped her head and sometimes recited along under her breath; he saw the straight part of her hair and her strong nose. Then he realized, with a sudden shock, that this was the girl who had grown up across the street. He remembered her quick temper and high, wicked laugh—once he watched her kick out the rent collector for asking for a bribe, and it was with the same laugh that she was now shooing away some dirty hooligans. Beware, his mother had said. She's much too conceited. She will make problems later on in life.

But this was not what he saw. He saw a shy and fearless girl whom he was sure he must marry. He fumbled up from the grass and introduced himself. Ma kept her eyes down, her lashes covering her gaze. Two hot coins seemed to burn her cheeks. She had never seen a boy so foolish and earnest.

Abba refused to eat for days unless his father inquired after her. Finally my grandfather relented, and their marriage was arranged. My parents agreed that it was a good thing, Abba picking someone like Ma who was not afraid. Abba always believed—even as the sky spits at you, or a drought cheats you of your crop, or the soldiers plunder your house, or the rent collector wants a bribe—you do the right thing. You have to stand for something, like Naseem. That's what he taught Aisha and me.

When we came to America, though, we didn't know what the right thing was. Here we lived with no map. We became invisible, the people who swam in between

other people's lives, bussing dishes, delivering groceries. What was wrong?

We didn't know. The most important thing, Abba
said, was not to stick out. Don't let them see you. But
I think it hurt him, to hide so much.

EIGHT

THE NEXT MORNING I'M WOKEN BY AISHA GRIPPING my shoulder. I huddle deeper in the quilt, pushing my knees into the warm cracks.

"Nadira, get up. Now."

It's mostly dark in the room, gray light filtering through the lace curtains, but I can see Aisha is dressed up in a blue shirt and a navy skirt. Her hair is freshly washed and oiled into a ponytail, and she's wearing gold studs in her ears. She looks so much older to me, and I feel even worse for what happened the day before.

She slaps the covers. "Come on, Fatso. Let's go."

"Where?"

"Just get dressed. I'll tell you later."

Here I was, feeling a little sorry for Aisha, and then she calls me names and bosses me around. Still, I hike myself out of bed and stumble into the bathroom, where I take a shower and put on the good clothes Aisha has handed to me.

"We're going to see Mr. Rashid ourselves," Aisha explains as we head toward the subway. "He has to get us out of this mess."

"What about school?"

"Don't be an idiot. This is much more important."

"But what if he won't see us?"

Aisha cocks her head to the side, and a wavy strand of hair falls across her cheek. "Not see us?" It's like it would never occur to her that she wouldn't get her way with Mr. Rashid.

There was only one time when I saw Aisha stumped. It was back in eighth grade when it was time to take the tests for Stuyvesant and Bronx Science, the magnet high schools. Aisha fell sick with a fever. For days Ma sat on a stool by her bedside pressing wet towels to her brow, but the fever raged hotter. Aisha began hallucinating, shouting out equations and vocabulary words. "Resuscitate!" she called, beating her fists into the mattress. "Infamy! Predilection!" After four days Abba wrapped her in a blanket and carried her in a taxi to the emergency room, where Aisha told the puzzled doctor: "Don't you dare keep me here on Saturday! That's my test day!"

The morning of the test Ma made her wear woolen stockings, a heavy coat, and a scarf, even though it was sixty degrees out. I thought Aisha was going to swoon. When the test results came, Aisha had missed getting in to both schools by a few points. She flung herself down on the bed and began punching the pillows. "It's not fair!" she sobbed. "It's just not fair!"

Today I watch Aisha stride ahead a few paces with her stern, determined gait. I've seen that look of hers before, and I know I have no choice but to follow her into the subway. We sit quietly on the train, comforted by the *click-clack* of the wheels, the swaying cars, and the view.

I love the 7 train. When we first moved here, Ma took me on a ride into the city. I'd never been on a train like this: It begins underground, then it shoots out of the tunnel high above the houses, rattling past them like a metal snake. I love that instant when we pull out of the underground tunnel into a blast of sunlight: It's like seeing a three-dimensional map laid out before you. We pass row after row of houses, each one of them filled with families like us, who came here and are starting again. Then the train speeds up, and the houses become taller apartment buildings and warehouses, and soon we're curving toward the city up ahead.

There are a lot of people in Mr. Rashid's waiting room today: some Indian lady with a briefcase and a Russian guy in a leather jacket who's talking on a cell phone. Even in our good clothes we seem out of place.

Ever since we came to America, there's been a chain of mistakes about our visas that has only gotten worse with time. First Abba found a lawyer to help us file for residency. Every time we visited his office, though, he kept losing our files or was confused about where things stood. One day when Abba called, his number had been disconnected. Soon after that, Abba received a letter from the government that said our lawyer was being investigated for fraud. Turned out the man made all kinds of mistakes, filing for people in ways that weren't allowed. Aisha saw Mr. Rashid on some TV show, and she was impressed, so she called him up and charmed him into being our lawyer. He agreed to take on our case, and lets us pay him slowly—fifty bucks here and there.

Mr. Rashid doesn't usually take on people like us. He works with people who have H-1B visas—guys who come here with computer and engineering degrees and have jobs. Mr. Rashid always dresses in fancy suits, and he has a gold chain around his wrist and a fat gold ring on his pinkie. He's light skinned, like a white man, and usually he greets us with this sturdy handshake that makes my elbow ache.

"You don't have an appointment?" his secretary asks. She's wearing a headset telephone and tips her chin up as if talking to the air.

"I left a message last night," Aisha replies. She adds, lowering her voice, "It's an *emergency*."

"We'll see if we can squeeze you in."

We sit and wait while people walk up to the secretary's desk, dressed smartly in suits, and down the carpeted hall. We wait some more. Aisha's foot jabs the swivel chair. I try doing some homework, then give up and flip through an old *Time* magazine. After about an hour Aisha asks how much longer it will be. "It's a busy day," the secretary replies. Another hour drags by. When we head over to the desk once more, the secretary looks up blankly from her computer screen. "I'm sorry. Mr. Rashid has lunch right now—"

Aisha pushes past the desk, through the swinging door. "You can't go in there!" But Aisha is already in Mr. Rashid's office—he's there, laughing, holding up his palms.

"The boat can't wait for the tide, nah?" he asks in Bangla.

I can tell Mr. Rashid is trying the uncle routine, asking after everyone. He offers us some caramels, but Aisha's furious, so I shake my head no.

"Aisha, Nadira. It's so good to see you. I'm glad you're carrying on normally. That's the most important thing right now."

Aisha's brow wrinkles; she pulls to the edge of her seat. "Mr. Rashid, let me get to the point. In two months I'm going to hear from colleges. I'm even up for valedictorian—"

"Congratulations! That's marvelous, Aisha!"

She gives him a cold look. "None of that matters anymore. Not if Abba is in detention. They've hauled him off as if he's a criminal or a terrorist or has something to hide. We have to clear up this whole business. So Ma doesn't have to live in a shelter, and I can go to college, and we can just *get on with our life.*"

A look of amazement floats across Mr. Rashid's face.

"Aisha," he says gently. "I wish I could tell you that Immigration cares about your grade point average. But this is very serious. Anyone who does not have legal status here does not have a right to a hearing. They can detain him as long as they like. Your father took a great risk when he went up to Canada. Once he tries to apply for asylum in another country, his application here is void."

"But we never even got that far! They arrested him instead!"

"Of course they did. He was re-entering with an expired visa."

"But what were we supposed to do? You said you didn't know if we'd ever get residency. And Tim told us, with the Special Registration it could be worse—"

"I know. But your father panicked."

Aisha sinks back. Was Mr. Rashid saying that we were to blame? "What are you saying?" she asks.

"You have no idea what a tall order it is, getting you folks out of this. It's a real mess."

We sit in silence for a few minutes. Mr. Rashid's bank of telephone buttons are bleeping and flashing. I notice all the folders in the usually neat office: stacked upon his desk, on the extra chairs. Our family is just one folder, I realize, and a not very important one.

Aisha doesn't seem to notice. "Then we have to clean it up," she persists.

"Aisha," Mr. Rashid laughs. "All the will in that seventeen-year-old body of yours could not clean up the messes at the INS."

"What are you saying?"

"I'm saying this is a process. You have to wait and see."

Aisha slams her knapsack down on the floor, and her hair springs out of her rubber band and swings across her face. I can see the startled, angry look on Mr. Rashid's face. Spoiled girl, he seems to be thinking. Impatient like all the Americans.

"Mr. Rashid," she says. "We hired you because we trusted you to do the best job you can." She holds an arm out toward his wooden door. "My parents may not be as educated or rich or as desirable as your other clients over there. But we count too."

Aisha opens the door and pushes into the corridor, past the bewildered secretary, out to the elevator, and downstairs. I run after her, barely able to keep up, weaving through the zigzagging commuters in Grand Central.

"He's not going to do anything for us," she says quietly. "We have to take care of it ourselves."

"What?"

"We're going to go to the authorities and show them it's a mistake."

"Are you kidding?" I almost laugh in disbelief, except there is nothing funny about this.

"Why not? I'm a good debater. I've argued these sorts of things before." She sounds almost cheerful. I've seen Aisha in this mood, ready to meet the challenge in front of her.

"But Aisha, you heard what Mr. Rashid said. It's a mess. *We* made the mistake. We have to wait and see—"

Aisha makes her eyes go small. "Nadira, the trouble with you is you don't fight. You just give in."

Backpack hitched over her shoulder, she heads toward the subway entrance. If it weren't for that hair of hers springing in angry coils around her shoulders, I would lose her in the crowds. By the time I catch up with her, I yank her arm, hard, toward me.

"You can't do that!" I yell. "You can't just run off. Or tell Mr. Rashid the first thing that comes into your head!" Then I notice that Aisha is trembling. Her backpack slides off her arm, and she slouches to the ground, right next to the Zaro's Bread barrel full of Snapple bottles banked in ice. Her eyes are glassy, far-off. I crouch down next to her. "Aisha, what's wrong?"

"I'm scared," she whispers. "I'm scared for Abba."

It's as if Aisha is finally saying what we're both afraid to imagine: Abba crouched in a cold dark cell. Abba sitting at some table with a ceiling lamp glaring down on his face. Are they badgering him with questions? Letting him sleep and bathe and pray? Beating him with a stick until the bruises show like dark flowers?

We don't know the answers to any of these questions, and as we make our way down the subway and onto the 7 train, it's like we keep seeing different versions of what's happening to Abba flash across the windows. Everything looks different to us now: the streets, the tar roofs, the park. I inch a little closer to Aisha. None of this is ours anymore, we realize, and for the rest of the ride we say nothing.

NINE

THE NEXT DAY AISHA AND I GINGERLY MAKE OUR way to school as if we're afraid that any minute now someone is going to tap us on the elbows and firmly lead us away. All through social studies class I keep having this weird vision of a police officer showing up at school. I see his visor tipping down as he pushes through the door. He and Mr. Laird huddle together, and then their eyes comb me over. The other kids are snickering, laughing, and my neck grows sticky with sweat as they pull me away from everything I know.

When we came back from the Canadian border, at first it wasn't so hard, keeping up. That's what we do all the time. We've always been told to never say a word about our status. We can have friends at school, even hang out after with them. But we were taught to keep to ourselves. Ma and Abba, even though they're not like some parents—they'd never show us a snapshot of a

boy we have to marry or stop us from going to college—
they have their ways. And that means: Never tell anyone
anything private about the family. Never air your troubles.
That would spoil our honor. I've never had a friend over
at our apartment—not even Lily.

Now it's not so easy keeping our trouble pressed
away, out of sight. I keep thinking about Aisha crouched
by the Zaro's barrel, looking so broken. It's lonely, doing
this. And Aisha, I realize, is the only one who will understand.

At lunch I search her out in the cafeteria. "Hey," I
say. "I'm sorry about yelling at you yesterday." She
looks skeptical, but I press on. "I was thinking. Maybe
you're right. Maybe we could figure this out ourselves."

She smiles wanly. "I actually do have an idea. About
what we can do."

After classes let out, we head over to Dunkin'
Donuts. While I make my way through two jelly doughnuts, Aisha, who has borrowed Risa's cell phone, calls
Tim's organization and the detainment center, and then
she gets a lawyer on the phone, and finally she even
speaks to an INS officer. Mostly they give her the
runaround, and each time she's put on hold she nervously squeezes crumbs between her thumb and fore-
finger and rubs them across her teeth. It sounds crazy,
two teenagers thinking they can argue their way into the
immigration department. But Aisha's got this fire in her.
It's different from Taslima's, which is more like a lot of
words that ignite and spark around us and fade out

once she's done yelling. Aisha's burns slow and steady.

Finally I say to her, "Don't you think we should call Ma? At least find out what she's heard."

Aisha slowly sets the phone down. This never occurred to her—calling our mother for something so simple as information. I think Aisha's afraid of upsetting Ma or making her feel worse about everything, especially since we moved to America and Ma's grown shy about her English.

The cell phone rings once, twice, and on the third ring Ma picks up.

"Oh, Nadira!" she cries. I keep seeing her in that crazy purple coat, sitting alone on an army cot.

"Hey Ma, have you heard anything more?"

"They've asked your father a lot of questions about money. You know, the way we keep our savings through Ali, your uncle—"

"Ali?" I can't believe it. Is that what he meant the other day when he stared so hard before turning down the block? Why didn't he explain himself then?

Ma's spirit seems to be flagging, and we reassure her that we're on the case, finding out what we can. "I taped the chocolate cake show for you," I tell her to make her feel better. "Auntie let me use her VCR."

"Did you get Emeril?" she asks. "He was supposed to do something with crabs."

"I'll get the rerun."

As I'm saying good-bye, we both look up to see Tareq sauntering over. He drops himself down at the table next to us, a doughnut in each hand. He's in a T-shirt, not even a jacket, though it's pretty cold out, and I can see the blue mark of a tattoo just under the edge of his sleeve.

"What do you want?" Aisha asks.

"Come on, Aish. I heard you over there. Trying to get your dad out of jail."

She stares at the papers spread on the Formica table.

"We *deshis*, we gotta help each other. One hand helps the other. Listen to me. All this stuff, talking to the authorities. It's cute and all. But *niger dom noshto ko'ro na*—don't waste your breath."

Aisha's chin juts out. Her eyes smolder.

"Look, I can take care of it if you want. It just takes a little help—"

"We don't need that kind of help, Tareq."

"Man! You Bangla girls. Always so stuck up. That's why I never go out with you all." He crumples his white paper bag and twists up from his seat. Still cursing, he slams out of the store. Through the windows I see there's a girl sitting in his car, a white girl with brown hair, checking her teeth in the mirror.

"Stupid," Aisha whispers under her breath.

"Aisha, he was just trying to help. In his own way."

"Right. You want to give him money for a fake ID? You know how much trouble we could get into? He's a creep, Nadira."

"But what if—what if he's right?" I stare at our notes

71

spread on the table. Suddenly it all looks silly to me, no more than a dumb class assignment, kid stuff. Tareq with his rough mouth and heavy workboots and strong arms—he seems real. Tareq goes into the night and cruises the neighborhood talking to men behind walls and on cell phones in secret places where grown-up business goes on.

Aisha's still gazing through the window. "There's got to be a way," she says quietly.

The mosque is dim and smells of leather and stale sweat. I push my scarf over my head and follow Aisha past the room where men are praying into a little office where Ali-Uncle is sitting at a desk.

When Aisha and I tell him about what's happened, his face goes very still. He presses his hands together in a bridge and sits for a few minutes, thinking. "I can't tell you how many of these stories I keep hearing. Every other day there's another man who comes in here, or a wife who doesn't know where her husband is."

"But what about the fund?"

"The other day the director handed over a list of names, especially those who had contributed to our fund. He had no choice, really."

"And what is this fund exactly?" Aisha asks.

"It's an account all us Bangladeshis keep, an association."

"What kind of association?" She's leaned forward,

her small pad of paper on her knees, scarf slipping behind her ears.

"We pool our money, and that way you can take out or borrow from it for important things, like starting a business. The Koreans do it, and you can see how well they've done."

"And how do you know whose money is whose?"

Ali-Uncle rolls back on his chair and opens a file cabinet. Inside, he fishes out a big dusty blue ledger. His finger trails down a list of names, each written in tiny print in black ink. "See there," he says. "This is your father's." When he turns the book around, I can see three thousand dollars listed, and then a smaller sum under INTEREST. "That's for college," he explains. "He kept putting it away, whatever he could. He was so proud that he could do that for the both of you."

The *both* of us? I think.

"He never told us," Aisha whispers.

"Of course not. He wanted to make sure he could start paying your fees in the fall, Aisha. And you, Nadira, he knew you weren't far behind, so he was working hard to cover you, too."

"But the whole idea was I would get a scholarship. That we'd be legal—"

He shrugs. "He knew that might not be possible. He wanted to do everything he could to make sure that you would never be disappointed."

For a few minutes we sit in silence, a dusty shaft floating through the window making it hard to see Ali-Uncle's face. I can see men in their skullcaps filing inside. I look over at Aisha and see that for once she's surprised too. But why did Abba hide this from us? How stupid, I think. Now those secrets are a misunderstanding, and it's ruining our whole lives.

"So you can write us a letter? Explaining everything?" Aisha asks.

"Of course. I will have the treasurer of the mosque sign it so it is official."

Ali-Uncle swivels around and rolls his chair toward a little table with an old computer. I have never seen a man so gentle. He moves slowly, as if no one, no problem, should ever hurry him. It almost hurts me to watch him flick on the computer, his long, slender fingers carefully tapping out his letter. He's so assured and graceful. It's like a precious vase that I'm afraid will break. I remember how he once came to our home, and Aisha and I were fighting over the TV, and he put a palm on each of our heads and said, "Do you think you will even remember that this matters tomorrow?" His hand on my head had made me suddenly sleepy and slow.

That night Aisha and I lock ourselves in Taslima's bedroom and stay up for hours planning our next step. We're going right to the top: We're going to write the new director of immigration and our congressman, pleading for special circumstances. Aisha has a whole argument mapped out—the mistake about the money, Abba who's worked so hard in this country, and about us, too, such good students who want to contribute something to America. (She has to fudge a little on my grades.)

Later Taslima comes in. She looks tired and I notice her spikey hair has been dyed two colors: orange and dark brown. When we tell her about our letter, she sniffs, making the tiny ruby chip in her nose glint. "You really think a letter is going to help?"

"Why not?"

"Oh please, guys." She hefts her black canvas bag onto the bed and pulls out a fluorescent green flyer.

PROTEST THE PERSECUTION

OF IMMIGRANTS!

NO SPECIAL REGISTRATION.

NO DEPORTATION.

RIGHTS FOR

IMMIGRANT WORKERS.

"That's what I've been doing," she explains. "I've been out there every day."

"What about school?"

"This is my education, Aisha." She grabs a stack and tosses them on top of our yellow pad. "That's what you should be doing. Not some little letter. This is political. And the only way to fight a political situation is to be political."

Aisha stares at the papers near her lap. I know what she's thinking: Abba would never allow us to go out in public like that and raise our voices. She tilts her head, chewing on the rubbery nub of her eraser. "You have to admit, Taslima. We've broken the law. Several laws, in fact."

Taslima's face darkens. "They didn't care about that before."

"If you're going to fight an enemy, you have to understand their argument. You can't just demand. That's not how you're going to win, Taslima. You have to make a good case. Like, if they let my family stay, I'll be going to college and making a contribution. Or that your Abba contributes all the time. Think of all those big fancy dinners that get pulled off in the city because of him. You have to speak to their fears. You can't harangue them into letting you in."

"But they did let us in!"

"Maybe. But there's a saying: 'Because we looked away in the past, does that mean we can look away now?'"

Taslima grabs up her flyer and shoves it in her black canvas bag. I see the hurt that puckers across Aisha's brow. "Come on, Taslima, let's not fight." She pulls close to her and smiles. "You know who we saw today?"

"Who?"

"Tareq. With the ugliest girl in his car."

Taslima grins. She thinks Tareq's a pea brain, dumb as can be. Soon the three of us are curled up on the bed talking. It's been so long since we've done this. Taslima gives us the gossip from Queens College, where there was some kind of poetry festival and another cousin of ours was skateboarding in the quad before it began and threw his back out. His mother is this awful lady who puts on airs and considers herself an important feminist poet. "You should have seen her—she wore this bright orange *shalwar kameeze* and kept reciting some awful verses about blood and oranges and childbirth. And there's Mahmoud in the first row, groaning and moaning. We were peeing in our pants, I swear." Aisha and I can't stop laughing, and the sounds widen, making bright circles in the room.

For the next few days that letter is all Aisha and I can think about. We talk about it on the way to school, jammed together on the crowded bus; we meet at lunchtime in the cafeteria, and late at night we stay up whispering with the lights out. We don't let Uncle or Auntie know, of course. When we hear from Ma—about how she only saw Abba for ten minutes and she's worried about running out of money—it only makes us more sure of what we're doing.

Besides the letter to our congressman and the Homeland Security director, Aisha's gotten on the phone and called Abba's boss and asked him to write a nice letter about Abba. We've even put in our school records to show what good kids we are, and Ali-Uncle has written a letter about the fund. Taslima scoffed at us when we decided to include this stuff. "These are stupid bureaucrats," she snapped. "Do you think they care about any of that?"

"We have to try," Aisha had calmly replied.

Ma found a copy shop in Burlington, where she's faxed over whatever papers she's gotten about Abba's detention. When we go to pick up the fax one afternoon at Tim's apartment, I'm amazed: There must be something like a dozen people in the cramped living room talking on cell phones, arguing. The coffee table is spilling over with flyers and dirty ashtrays and coffee cups; sheets hang cockeyed on the windows. I'm surprised to see that Taslima is so at home here: She sits cross-legged on the futon couch and greets everyone as if this is her place.

For the first time I notice the resemblance between Tim and Taslima: They both have these skinny bodies and short hair that stands up on end. Tim is always doing ten things at once, although every now and then, he'll stop and let his hand rest on Taslima's hip, and the two of them will look at one another with a stillness between them that makes me sad and happy.

It's been a long while since I felt so good about Aisha. We're together, a sister-sister team. Sometimes an idea occurs to me in the middle of class, and I'll jot it down and meet her in the halls later. Papers we can show. A way to phrase something. It's like my brain is suddenly sharp and clear, though I'm moving real slow, and I know what my move is two steps ahead of me. Aisha is the one who can flash with quick ideas, but sometimes she gets overexcited and stressed out, and she loses track of what she's trying to say.

I think about what Ma said, how I'm patient and that one day people will see my slow, steady strength. And I keep thinking about Ali-Uncle, how he never hurries himself, and he always knows in advance what he's going to do or say. He once told me that every action, every word of his, is watched by Allah. If I say a word that is angry, he explained, then I should never be surprised by the harm. And if I say something good, then it is like watching my own garden grow, and that is the greatest pleasure ever. That's what Aisha and I are doing. We're planting a garden with our words. Our future. Everything careful and chosen well so the shoots come up strong and straight. It's as if Ali-Uncle's hands are still on our heads, warming us from the inside out.

TEN

THE BANGING STARTS SLOW AT FIRST. I'M DREAMING about sitting by a river and a boat knocking against wood. *Thud-thud.* Faster, louder. Voices rippling up from below.

Spider-crabs of light crawl across my lids, then I'm sitting up in bed, all the lamps blazing on. Uncle lumbers across the room in his pajamas followed by Auntie cinching her robe tight. "Don't let them in," she whispers.

"Who is it?" he shouts.

"Immigration, sir. May we please come in?"

"No!" Auntie whispers.

Uncle has already thrown back the latch. Three people peer from the doorway—two men and a woman in a raincoat. The tall man reminds me a little of Tim, though he holds himself a little stiffly and flashes a silver badge in a slim black case. The other man is young and is wearing a quilted vest. I've only ever seen one of those on TV.

"Sir, we're here to ask you a few questions."

"What questions?" Uncle's voice wobbles.

"Please don't be frightened, sir. It's just a routine check."

The woman pushes forward. She's short and plump and pats the rumpled pockets of her coat. "Can we see your documentation?" she asks.

"No!" Taslima's wedged between them, cell phone clutched in her hand. "We don't give any papers without our lawyer present."

An annoyed look twitches across the man's face. "If you've got nothing to hide—"

"Do you have a warrant?" She holds up her cell phone. "If you'd like to wait, I can call my lawyer."

The man takes a step back. Clearly he's surprised at the way she's speaking in such clear, commanding English.

"We'll have to ask you to come to the station house."

Uncle is standing near the door, frozen. His arms hang at his sides at this crazy crooked angle, and his eyes glitter like black stones. It's like the words are stuck in his mouth, and he can't get them out. One part of him wants to answer the man, I can see, and the other is being tugged back to Taslima. I know he hates this: He hates that his English has fled him, and his own daughter is showing him up in front of an American man.

"Sir—," he begins.

"Abba, no—"

She's stepped in front of Uncle now. But Uncle is furious—he pushes her aside and walks toward the man. "Sir, if you please. Can you leave my home?" The way he says the word *home* has a certain tinge; it's the way he would say it in Bangla, that means this place that is my family's, that only invited guests may enter.

The man looks startled. He shakes his head. "Mr. Rahman. The thing is this. If you come down with us to the station house and answer our questions, it will be much better."

His words hang in the air, vibrating like an electric wave. We know what they mean. *You're illegal, and we can push this further. Don't make a fuss. We hold the cards.*

Taslima raises her cell phone as if it's some super-bionic zap gun that can make these guys disappear. But they don't disappear. The woman slips inside and puts a hand on Auntie's arm, whispering softly to her, "Just put on your coat, ma'am. It won't take very long."

I chew on my thumbnail. I don't like this woman touching Auntie.

"Don't panic," Taslima pleads in Bangla. "Please, just call Tim. He'll tell us what to do."

"Tim!" Uncle whispers. "Why should I listen to that *shada-chele*? Isn't it he who sent my sister and brother-in-law up to Canada? Such a foolish chase that was! And now this."

Then Uncle turns to the tall man, and I see how all the fierceness has drained from him. His hands tremble as he shrugs on his coat. He dips his head as he's led out the door as if he's afraid to stand too tall.

When Tim joins us at the police station and hears that Uncle's already gone in for questioning, he slaps his hands against his legs. "Oh, great."

"I told you not to talk to them without a lawyer," Taslima says to Auntie, who is sitting on the hard bench, her hands squeezed together.

"Hush, young lady. You don't know everything. What if your father were to defy them?"

"But this is just stupid. Tim is trying to help. And now you go and do this."

"He's not family," Auntie replies. "He shouldn't be here." She crosses her arms across her chest, staring dully ahead.

Tim has gone into a glass partitioned area. He's talking rapidly, but it doesn't seem to be doing much good. The officers stay behind their desks and shrug. Like Taslima, Tim uses his cell phone to point and gesture, jabbing the air, but eventually they turn away. I look at the wall clock: It's four in the morning. Aisha is already curled up in a seat using her jacket as a pillow.

"Taslima, if your Tim wants to do some good, he should take these children home," Auntie says. "They don't need to stay here."

Aisha sits upright. "I'm staying," she says flatly.

Taslima flips open her cell phone and punches in

some numbers. It doesn't work. She shakes the phone, dials again, curses under her breath.

"Taslima!" Auntie gives her a warning look.

A woman officer strolls up to us. "Can't call in the station house!" she barks.

"What if I'm trying to reach my lawyer?"

"Can't use cell phones here." The officer is plump, like the other woman, and her blue uniform pants fan into creases around her hips.

"So what am I supposed to do?" Taslima asks.

The officer regards her as if testing the space between them, judging whether she should even bother to help Taslima. The more Taslima talks, the worse she makes things with her agitated, angry air. Aisha shifts up from her seat, tucks her hair behind her ears, and speaks very softly.

"If you please, miss," she says. "We don't know the rules. We've never been in a station house before. Can you tell me where we are allowed to make phone calls?"

The officer softens a bit. Her gaze slides back to Taslima with her punky short hair sticking up like bristles, her wiry, tense body. Then she regards Aisha, who is standing with her ankles pressed together, chin tipped up, showing the wide planes of her cheeks. I know this look in Aisha: it's the girl who knows how to please everybody to get what she wants.

"Call out in the hall," the woman suggests.

Smiling, Aisha asks quietly, "And, please, can I speak to your supervisor?"

The woman officer squints. "What for?"

She gives her another sweet smile. "So we understand the procedures."

A few minutes later another woman with pens clipped to her front pockets arrives. "Yes?" she asks.

Aisha first rolls up her sleeves to her elbows before speaking. Then she starts to talk quietly. "Please, miss," she begins. "I understand that you're just doing your job. But there is a larger issue here. My uncle being held like this, it's a violation of his civil liberties—"

"Honey, your uncle don't even have his papers right. What kind of liberties you think he has?"

Aisha's head tilts back as if the woman has slapped her lightly. Then I see her eyes grow firm again. "Any individual, from any country, no matter what their immigration status, has a right to a lawyer—"

"Save it," the woman interrupts. "You want to talk about rights, you don't have a right to sit in this area. We're just tryin' to make it easier for you folks."

The woman turns away, her gun creaking on its holster.

We wait. For a long time. Officers go back and forth in the corridor, folders tucked beneath their arms. We drink coffee and sip Cokes from the machine until our hands jump and twitch. The fluorescent bulbs buzz overhead.

At seven in the morning a new officer comes out. This one is a man with a Spanish name on his tag and black curly hair.

"My husband?" Auntie asks, half rising from her chair.

He spreads his hands. "I'm sorry, ma'am. But your husband is being moved to a facility in Manhattan."

"You are taking my husband to jail?"

When he nods, Auntie lets out a wail like I've never heard, pulling at her own cheeks. My heart feels as if it's been twisted into a knot.

We try everything. Aisha argues with the policeman, fingers hooked around her jeans belt. But he just explains it's out of his jurisdiction, the FBI has taken over these cases, so that's why they're taking Uncle to a federal center. We try to make a few phone calls, but since it's so early no one is at their office. By now we know Uncle is gone—handcuffed and strapped into a van and driven over the Queensborough Bridge.

Outside it's like we're landing on an outer-space planet. Our legs are loose kneed and weak. The streets are soaked in a frosty white light.

Auntie, her pocketbook clutched against her hip, keeps turning in circles as if she's not sure which way to go first. Gently, Taslima takes her by the arm and leads her to a diner on the corner. We're all ravenous. We order fried eggs and potatoes and pancakes, and cup after cup of thin coffee. I don't remember ever seeing Auntie sitting at a place like this before. But eating is all we can do so the night is pushed from our minds.

Aisha shoves her plate aside and starts to cry. "It's all my fault. I should have been able to convince them to let Uncle out."

Auntie puts a hand on hers. She's pulled herself together, though her eyes are glassy. "No, no, that's not true."

"Aisha, you're nuts," Taslima puts in. "Those people in there are fascists. They don't give a damn about listening to anyone."

Aisha is sobbing harder now. "No, you're wrong. I should have convinced them. If only I'd said the right thing. If only I said more—"

No matter what we tell Aisha, she won't listen. She sobs harder and harder, her back banging against the cushioned booth.

Back at the apartment I'm so tired I don't even pull out the sofa bed, but drop down on the cushions, still in my clothes. A sour-ash taste coats my mouth.

The garbage truck roars by. I can hear voices in the kitchen, Auntie and Taslima arguing softly. Aisha is making her way across the living room, a blanket wrapped around her and trailing along the floor. After the apartment is quiet again, I realize the thud-thudding noise hasn't gone away. It's my own heart, beating fast in my chest.

ELEVEN

WE'VE BECOME A HOUSE RUN BY WOMEN. JUST like Uncle warned.

We've done all we can. Called Mr. Rashid dozens of times until his voice grew thin and exasperated. Stood outside the detention center in Manhattan, knuckles chafed, cheeks sliced with cold, until they sent us home saying there's nothing more we can do. Then we come back to the empty apartment, blinking, as if surprised not to see Uncle running his bristle brush over his shoes or gargling in the bathroom. Auntie leaves in the morning for her cashier's job at the ninety-nine cent store, and we take off soon after, our nylon backpacks lumpy with books. I notice fewer and fewer chunks of fish in our gravy, and Auntie waits until the market is closing to buy the vegetables spotted brown and marked down to half price. Nights, she curls up on the sofa in front of the TV with a milky tea on her lap, absently patting the cushions.

Yet I can feel Uncle and Abba, like shapes behind the walls. I see Uncle's black trousers with the satin stripes hanging in the closet and Abba's exam books stacked beneath, the ones he always hoped to review to get a new degree. I feel them in the empty rooms: their heavy-sweat smell, the rumble-sound of their voices.

A few days after Uncle was put in detention, Aisha and I go to the library, where we sign up for a computer to type out our letters to Homeland Security and other officials. We have to wait a whole hour to get on, and when we do get our turn, it takes a long time because the printer keeps jamming and the librarian is too busy to help us. Aisha does a few searches and gets the right addresses; then we slip the letters into their envelopes and take them to the post office, where we send everything certified mail.

When we're done, we celebrate with milk shakes and red-bean buns, my favorite next to jelly doughnuts. "Isn't it cool?" I say to Aisha and squeeze her hand.

She can only manage a weak smile. "Since when did you become such a rah-rah cheerleader, Nadira?"

A hotness burns my cheeks. "I don't know. I guess before . . ." I pause. "Before, you always took over, Aisha. It's like you didn't leave any room for me."

For an instant Aisha's eyes flash, and I'm sure she's going to say something mean, put me down. Instead she laughs and picks up the rest of her bun. "There's plenty of room, Nadira. You just have to learn how to grab it."

After that, something shifts between Aisha and me. It's like she's opened the door and wriggled over to let me into her private little world. I know Lily's hurt because I keep avoiding her. I barely talk to her in math class. I barely talk to her at all, especially since stuff at her house is getting crazy again. But it's fun hanging with Aisha. I feel a little like a spy, sitting with her friends in the cafeteria, listening to them talk about scholarships at Wellesley and the University of Pennsylvania, or about "senior year slog." With these guys that usually means an *A-*. A real joke.

"Guess what!" It's a Friday, and Kavita is leaning over, hands flat on the Formica table. "Last night my parents told me about my graduation present. I'm going to India to see my grandparents and they're going to take me to Rajasthan and we're going to stay in a big palace hotel!"

"Wow," Risa says.

Aisha stares down at her hands, her expression suddenly sad. Since we're illegal we never get to go back to Bangladesh. We talk to our grandparents once a month on a phone card, and their voices sound far away, as if they could fade into the wire.

Everyone starts chattering about summer plans. Risa is going to a special music camp for really serious violinists. Rose has some kind of internship at a hospital. It's all so senior-year normal, even though everyone has the jitters, not knowing where they'll be next year.

Nothing like what we wonder.

I look over at Aisha, who's nervously palming her hair down. That's when I realize Aisha let me into her life because she's feeling left out of her own. She's known these girls since freshman year; they're like a tribe that's stuck together. They've climbed up all the honors and AP classes together, swapping notes, doing study sessions. It's from them that Aisha figured out how to be the girl she became—how to stay smart, what words to use, how to act in the school halls, especially when the tough girls give her a hard time for being so smart. But now she's not the same as they are; she's falling away into a corner. And she only feels safe with me, who knows what's really going on.

At first I'm angry, knowing that she's using me. Then I feel bad for her. Aisha's always so worried about what her friends will think. Maybe that's the good thing about not being popular: I don't even know what others think about me. It's easier for me to say what I think since it's not so mixed up with other people's ideas. I'm not afraid of how stupid I sound. I feel especially sorry for Aisha when she chimes in boastfully, "Talk about senior year slog. You want to know what I did today? I got a C in American government."

They all stare at her, surprised.

"Are you serious?" Kavita asks.

"Yes." Her voice is tiny, as if she's swallowed it.

I can tell from the puzzled looks on their faces. Aisha's boast isn't funny; it's just kind of weird, especially among these guys.

That night I hear Aisha whispering to herself, scolding. "I keep thinking of that night at the police station. With Uncle. If I'd said it differently—" She sighs. "I can't focus on anything anymore."

I put a hand on her wrist. It feels clammy and warm. Now I'm really sorry for Aisha. She's starting to wear herself down.

The next day she shows up at lunch looking a little odd, like she's worked too hard at her appearance. Her hair has been slicked back into a ponytail and she's wearing a shirt that's starched and buttoned to her neck, even though it's warm out. Her face seems as if it was coated in a waxy polish, and her eyes are a little too bright. She starts talking about her special interview at Barnard, how it's all going to work out. "They wouldn't bother if they weren't thinking of giving me a lot of money," she tells the others. "I know it." She says this five or six times, sounding like a windup doll, and Risa and the others keep giving each other funny looks.

On the way back from school Aisha repeats to me, "We're going to hear from the lawyer, Nadira. Today. Or our letter, it's going to be answered. I know it."

But when we get to the mailbox, it's empty. And there are no messages on the machine.

Aisha becomes obsessed. Every day there's no letter in the mailbox from Homeland Security, no phone call from the lawyer. Every evening that we speak to Ma and hear there's no news there, either, Aisha grows more frantic. At night she goes over her homework again and again.

She gets up early to go to school, studying in the empty classrooms. She's like a boxer, jabbing and hitting, trying her old moves, but this time she's up against something that's so much bigger than her, beyond her power.

I wish I could just put a hand to her skin, stop her whirring inside.

Soon Aisha is barely going out. She sits in Taslima's room and stares out the window. Her hair looks greasy; she hasn't even bothered to press coconut oil into her scalp or run her fingers through the kinks. She keeps wearing that stupid Destiny's Child T-shirt, and when no one's home, she sneaks into the living room and watches soaps on TV.

She goes to school, but it's like she's hardly there. I don't know if she shows up for her after school stuff. And I'm tired of the lies—to Mr. Friedlander, to her friends, to our parents. Every day is a piece of rubber stretched so tight it's going to snap. Aisha's gang tries to find out what's happening. But Aisha starts avoiding them. At lunch she gulps down her food and then leaves, says she has to go study.

"What is going on?" Risa asks us once after school. "I tried calling you the other day, and the number didn't work—"

"I've been busy," Aisha replies and starts walking down the steps.

"Aisha!" Kavita calls out. "What about Saturday?" It's the city-wide debate team finals, and all the participating schools will be at the Marriott in Manhattan.

Aisha keeps walking, her elbows pressed at her sides.

The next morning Aisha wakes up late and stays in bed. She doesn't even try to get dressed to go on the subway to Manhattan for the city-wide rounds. Around midday she rouses herself, a blanket wrapped around her. "You have a cold?" Auntie keeps asking. Aisha shakes her head. She shuffles back into Taslima's bedroom, shutting the door softly. A few times I think I hear the sound of her crying.

That night Aisha and I sleep hunched against one another. I can sense her fright, her cold heels bumping against mine. "Go to sleep," I tell her over and over, but I know she can't.

Taslima starts to slip away too. More and more she stays out late and doesn't even apologize when she sneaks back in, shoes in her hand. Auntie begs her, "Please tell me where you are going all these crazy hours."

Taslima pushes her fists into her leather jacket. "Ma, you know where. We've got work to do. The protest."

"Your father, if he knew—"

"My father's in jail! Why do you think I'm doing this?"

"But to go out on the streets, so brazenlike—"

"Amma."

Taslima's grabbed Auntie by both arms, and she's holding her, shaking her firmly, as if Auntie is the child and she's the stern grown-up. "Amma, this is what they want. For us to be afraid."

That evening Taslima pulls me into her bedroom. She's all hollows and scooped out shadows. A blue bead strung on a silver wire gleams against her thin neck. She's cut her hair even shorter, so it sticks up from her scalp like thin black needles. "I know Abba would be upset," she whispers. "But I can't do it. I can't pretend like everything's normal." She clutches my hand. "Promise me, Nadira, that you won't let Ma know I'm not going to classes."

"But what if you get kicked out?"

She looks at me, hard. "I could get thrown out of this country any day now." She turns away, chewing on her lip as if she already has another life elsewhere. It scares me, what Taslima is doing. Taking her anger outside for all the world to see, like turning open our skins, raw and ugly.

And me, I don't know what to do with myself anymore. I can't figure out how to get us through this—to pick up the thread of working together, to continue our fight. None of it seems possible. Sometimes I'll pull out the file and look at all Aisha and I did, and it feels silly, like a pretend social studies exercise. A baby thing.

I stop helping Ali-Uncle at the shop, telling him I have too much homework. I duck out of school through a different door so Lily won't find me. I feel guilty, but I just need to be alone. Not with her, or my sister, or anybody.

I don't know what I'm trying to find out, but it's inside me, somewhere.

Most of the time I take the subway to a different stop and wander around the neighborhood. Sometimes I go all the way to Seventy-fourth Street and stuff my face with *bhel pooris*, watching the mothers push their metal carts, the men stopping off at the video shop, listening to Hindi film music. It makes me miss Abba and Ma; we used to come here on Sundays, where she would fill up a basket with eggplants and long beans and sacks of rice. After shopping we'd eat at the $7.95 buffet, and Abba would promise to buy Amma a new set of gold bangles for her next birthday.

One day Lily finds me at my new secret exit door. "Nadira, why are you avoiding me?"

Her round face looks drawn, her eyes red rimmed. Suddenly I feel terrible. That's exactly what I've been doing—ducking from her.

"I'm sorry. It's just there's a lot happening. What's going on with you?"

"It's gotten worse," she tells me. "My mom says she's going to throw my dad out. And my dad's really upset; he can't even eat. You should see him, Nadira. Sometimes he works until two in the morning, and then she's at him first thing, yelling."

"Maybe your dad *did* do something wrong," I offer.

She looks at me, confused. "But he's such a great person."

Then she begins to cry again, and I'm confused

inside myself, too, about my own father. I miss Abba so much, but sometimes I get angry at him for putting us through all this. Why did he even bring us to America without the right papers? Then I think of him sitting alone in some dark cell, and I feel these broken pieces piercing my insides.

"Listen, Lily," I say, putting a hand on her arm. "If you could find out the real truth about your dad, would you want to know? Even if it hurts?"

Lily hesitates, her brow puckered. Then she nods, tears streaking down her face.

I tell Lily to meet me in two hours at Dunkin' Donuts, and I walk away, fast. I know what I have to do. It's like putting together two different versions of a story, or poring over a map, and then checking it out against the real place, puzzling out the whole picture.

It's a warm day, and I head to Main Street, where I'm going to spy on the manicurist that works in Lily's father's shop. I buy myself a Coke and a red-bean bun from the Chinese baker and wait by the cars. Inside I can see the manicurist sitting on a stool, lathering up customers' ankles, carefully brushing polish on their toes. She moves quickly and efficiently, and whenever there's a lull she comes outside to smoke a cigarette.

When her shift is done, she shrugs on a light raincoat. I follow her as she saunters down some side streets. There's a springy tilt to her walk.

She disappears into the side door of a house. I can see frilly curtains in the basement window. A few minutes later an old lady comes out buttoning her coat, holding a net bag of oranges.

I get up my nerve and press the buzzer. When the manicurist comes to the door, I'm surprised because she looks so young—she could be sitting next to Aisha in school. "Yes?" she asks. She's wiping her hands in a towel. I can tell her English isn't so good.

Quickly I pull out a folder from school. "I'm selling cookies," I lie. "For the Girl's Club."

A wail starts up from inside, and the manicurist turns away, distracted. I follow her into a tiny apartment that's close and warm. Pipes run across the low ceiling. There's a small kitchenette, the counter lined with freshly washed baby bottles on paper towels. Toys are scattered all over the floor, and so is an open package of diapers.

The manicurist pushes through a doorway hung with a curtain, jiggling the baby. It's then that I notice the photographs propped up on a shelf: her and Lily's dad holding hands in front of a restaurant; Lily's dad and the baby, sitting on a futon couch—the only piece of furniture in the room. Something catches in my throat. I feel as if I'm going to get sick, with the smell of steam and milk from the baby.

"Sell cookies?" the manicurist repeats. The baby lets out another shriek. Her cheeks are plump and flushed red. Weirdly, she reminds me a little of Lily.

"That's okay," I say, backing out. "I'll come back another time."

Once outside I lean over on the pavement taking gulps of fresh air. I start to walk fast, past the people streaming off the subway, up Northern Boulevard to Dunkin' Donuts. Lily is there doing her homework, a bag of doughnuts on the table. I cram a cinnamon one into my mouth and tell her—all in a rush—because I know I'll get sick if I stop. As Lily listens, her face crumples and tears start spilling out of her eyes.

After she's done crying, Lily puts her hand on mine. "Thanks, Nadira. You're the only one I know who could have done what you did. Figured all that out."

I don't know what she means exactly. I only know that these doughnuts aren't making me feel better and that I'm sick of knowing too much about the adults. It's not such a great talent, I think, this putting things together. Not if it makes people so sad.

"Where were you?" Auntie demands when I walk in the door. The lights are turned off, and it doesn't look like Aisha is home. I look guiltily at my feet. Does she know that I skipped out on Ali-Uncle and lied to that poor manicurist?

"Hurry now. We have to go. Your uncle, they're letting him out." She hands the phone receiver to me. "Call Mr. Rashid. He'll explain everything."

When I call Mr. Rashid, his secretary puts me right through. "They're releasing your uncle," he explains. "No charges filed. But he only has thirty days to resolve his immigration status. Otherwise deportation proceedings will begin." He pauses. "I'll tell you honestly, Nadira. These days I can't get anything done in thirty days with the INS."

"Does my aunt know this?" I ask.

"Not yet. She was just so excited about his release, I didn't want to upset her all over again."

I hang up and Auntie arranges for a driver from a cousin's company to drive us in his livery car to Brooklyn, where they've moved Uncle. We're silent the whole way, the blue-black air skimming past the windows. Auntie stays hunched against the door, her coat bunched thickly on her lap. We pull up to a dark building behind a huge wire fence. "You stay here," she instructs me and hurries inside. I wait for a long time, staring at the back of the driver's head. He's busy talking on his cell phone and ignores me. It's started to rain, and the windows are smeared and wet. My stomach hurts as if it's weighted down. I keep feeling guilty, though for what I'm not sure.

Two blurred shapes move out of the front doors, veering around the puddles: Auntie holding up a thin, wobbling Uncle. He's still in the same clothes he wore that night, his winter coat thrown over his shoulders. As they come closer, I see a limp in his walk.

The silence in the car is even worse on the way back. All I hear is the sound of the wipers thumping against wet glass. That and Uncle coughing spittle into a handkerchief.

"Taslima home yet?" he asks when he steps inside the apartment.

"No," Auntie replies. "Soon, though."

He pinches his mouth. "Where did she have to go that was so important, the first day her father is back?" Suddenly he whirls around and spots Aisha, who is frozen in the middle of the room. She keeps staring at Uncle as if he's a ghost that's returned, one of the shapes that's melted through the walls again. He looks different: his wrists jut out, and his skin is ashy and yellow.

"What are you staring at?" he shouts.

Still Aisha doesn't move.

"Stupid girls. All of them. Nobody listens."

He drops down on the sofa and switches on the TV with the remote. As he watches, I notice bruises and cuts on his forearms.

"I don't know what's wrong with him," Auntie whispers to us in the kitchen. "He doesn't talk. He just keeps asking for Taslima."

It's late when Taslima finally comes in. Aisha and I are already in bed trying to fall asleep. Tomorrow is Aisha's interview at Barnard, and she's lying rigid on the sheets, eyes bright, cheeks flushed. I squeeze her arm, but she barely moves.

It's weird. Now it's me who feels older than Aisha and is worried about her. Now that I've helped Lily, it's as if I want to protect everyone: Auntie from Uncle and the bad news about his possible deportation, Uncle from himself, and Aisha from taking everything so hard.

"Will you let me go with you?" I ask. I keep thinking if I can get to her, even make her say something mean, we can go back to the way it was before.

"I guess," she replies. She sounds distracted, more interested in the sounds coming from Auntie and Uncle's bedroom.

Uncle's voice is strange—not angry, as it usually is, but bitter.

"Tell me, Abba," I hear Taslima say.

"What is there to tell? They humiliated me. A grown man. They put lights on my face for hours. They gave me no food. They treated me like a liar." He sighs. "I was lucky. So many, they stayed for a long time now."

I can feel Aisha stiffen beside me, straining to hear what Uncle's saying. The endless, stupid questions. The cold cell and the toilet, filthy inside. "I was lucky," he keeps repeating. "They let me go early. I was lucky."

That night Aisha yells out in her sleep. She thrashes beside me, her hair springing up in wild coils. Her eyes look strange and unmoored. "What is it?" I ask.

"I keep having this dream," she whispers. "Every time I go up on the stage, these policemen come and tell me, 'You don't belong here.' Then they take me and lock me up in a cell with no light."

I pat her arm. "It sounds awful. But it's only a dream. No one's going to take you away. Come on, you're a star. You're going to do great."

"Maybe I shouldn't go tomorrow."

"Of course you should." I touch her shoulder. "I'll be there too."

She leans back on the pillows. "I'm so tired," she sighs. "So very tired."

TWELVE

BARNARD DOESN'T LOOK ANYTHING LIKE THE COLLEGE campuses in the brochures. You walk out of a dirty subway station to drab buildings on Broadway. Everything looks small and cramped. The stores and newsstands are no different than in our neighborhood, except the bus stops and wooden posts are plastered with flyers advertising rooms to sublet, yoga classes, furniture.

Aisha's skin is a pale oatmeal color, and she looks queasy, like she's going to bend over and get sick any minute. Since we still have a little time, we decide to take a walk. We pass a noodle shop full of students bent over big bowls of steaming soup.

"You want to eat?" I ask her.

"No." All morning she's been moody and quiet. She lurches off the curb, across the street, and leans against a post. "I don't feel so good," she groans.

"Maybe it's because you didn't sleep that much. Aisha, you've got to forget about everything that's going on at home. Abba would be upset if you let it get to you."

She nods weakly, her hand over her stomach. I touch her brow. It feels clammy. "Breathe," I tell her. "Just take long, deep breaths."

We walk around for a while on Broadway, then go down a steep side street to Riverside Park, where Aisha sits on a bench and rubs her palms on her knees. Later, when we reach the building for her interview, Aisha suddenly turns around and gently pushes me back. "Don't come in," she tells me. "It makes me too nervous. Why don't you meet me here in an hour?" She holds out her book bag full of all the stuff she's supposed to read for tomorrow.

"Okay, I guess."

I take the bag and stand there for a few more minutes while Aisha hurries up the steps and goes inside. Her coat flares open as she grabs the heavy door and swings it open. Then she's disappeared. It makes me a little sad watching her—like she's already gone from us.

A warm breeze is blowing off the river, so I decide to walk around by myself. I head across Broadway through the gates of Columbia, which open to a huge grassy courtyard. Two guys are tossing a Frisbee in the air. They look so natural, so at home. To my left is a set of stairs leading to a domed building. Everywhere I see girls a little older than Aisha walking past in jeans and cotton skirts. They're carrying books and talking to each other, going to important classes as if it's the most normal thing in the world.

I sit on the steps and watch kids carrying their cotton gym bags or dragging heavy book bags. Next to me is an Asian girl in a ribbed top and a cotton skirt that floats around her legs. She's holding a big sketch pad of drawings. I look closer and see that the page has wavy lengths of color broken up by jagged lines.

"What's that?" I ask.

"It's a glacier rock formation." When she sees my confused expression, she adds, "For my geology class. This is the structure of rock beds in Inwood Park."

"Cool. Does everybody have to do that?"

She shrugs. "Not really. But it's my major. I'm going to be a geologist. This summer I'm going to work out in Arizona and live in a tent and collect rock samples for this research lab."

I look at her, amazed. She's American-born. I can tell by her accent and the way she holds herself. I didn't even know you could do something like that. I sure didn't know a *girl* could do something like that.

"But how do you know you want to be a geologist?" I ask.

She smiles, tilting her head to the side. "How old are you?"

"Fourteen." I puff my chest out a little. "I'm in ninth grade."

"Well, when I was your age, I was always doing stuff with rocks. My knapsack used to weigh a ton from all the specimens I would carry around. In high school everyone thought I was kind of a freak. 'Rock Girl,' they'd call me. But around here people think it's okay. That's what's so cool about college, you know? You have a million kids doing all kinds of weird things here. My roommate's in this really wild band that only plays on the Internet. And there's this guy down the hall and he spent his spring break walking around Laos taking pictures."

"Wow." I always thought of college as a place for stars like Aisha, who does everything that her teachers expect from her, even down to hanging out in the right cliques. And all of us can see her there as clearly as if we had a TV screen of her life at school playing in our heads. But for the first time I start to actually imagine me sitting on concrete steps like this, or in a class reading lots of fat books and saying what I think. It suddenly feels as natural as sitting next to this girl, who is back to drawing with her colored pencils.

Her gaze is now on the guys whose Frisbee game has drifted nearer to us. The Frisbee lofts into the air, a disk of shining plastic. Then it starts its descent, and I glance at my watch and realize it's time to go get my sister. "Nice talking to you," I say, and get up to leave.

Back at Barnard I find Aisha not far from the front gate, bent over, vomiting onto the grass. When she lifts her face, the whites of her eyes are yellow and bloodshot.

"You okay?" I ask.

She shakes her head yes.

"You sure?"

She wipes her mouth and stuffs the tissue in her jacket pocket. "I'm all right now."

I don't know what to do. We start walking to the subway. "So how'd it go?" I ask.

"Okay." But she doesn't say anything more.

I decide to press her. "Did they give you an idea that you might be accepted?"

"They don't say things like that. It's just a lot of stupid questions. Nothing important." Slouching in her seat, she grabs her book from her bag and opens it. I notice, though, that she's not really reading. She's just staring dully at the page.

Monday morning we're walking to our homerooms when Mr. Friedlander comes striding right up to Aisha. He looks pissed—really pissed.

"Aisha!" he calls out.

Aisha turns, her books clasped against her chest.

"What's going on? You missed the city-wide finals a couple of weeks ago. Then you didn't even show for practice this Saturday!"

She tenses. "I was sick."

"And you couldn't have called?"

Aisha tucks her hair behind her ears. She gives him one of her sweet smiles. "I'm really sorry, Mr.

Friedlander. I was in bed all day with some kind of bad stomach flu. My ma says it's the fish she bought." She pauses. "And I've been thinking. Maybe I shouldn't be on the debate team anymore." She adds quietly, "My parents. You know, they're kind of old fashioned. And they don't like me going out so much. Especially with boys on the team."

I feel as if there's something shaking hard and loose in my stomach. How can you do this? I want to shout at Aisha. I've never heard her lie so much, right to someone's face. And about Ma and Dad, who aren't like what she's saying at all. The first time Aisha came home crying from grade school because the kids were making fun of her head scarf, Ma said firmly, "Don't wear it, then." Ma got a lot of flak from her friends for that and for other choices she made with Aisha, like letting her go on an overnight trip to Washington, D.C. "Let them peck like old chickens," Abba laughed. "We know who we are."

But it's like Aisha had this speech all prepared for Mr. Friedlander, this big fat lie. He takes a step back, a crease between his eyebrows. "But that's the whole point. The debate team. Your applications. You're even jeopardizing your valedictorian nomination." He puts his hands on his hips. "You want me to talk to your parents?"

She shakes her head firmly. "No. I'm really sorry, Mr. Friedlander. I appreciate your help."

She takes me by the arm and steers me around the corner, past the lockers, and toward the library.

"What did you do that for?"

She drops her hand. "Why bother? We're probably not even staying in this country. I don't want anyone to know what's going on with Abba."

"But what about the letters we sent? Why let everything go when there's still a possibility—"

She cuts me off. "Now he thinks it was Ma and Abba who prevented me from going. This way he won't think I'm a flake, which would be worse."

"But you lied. You lied about them!"

Her eyes get small. "Sometimes you have to," she mutters, and walks down the hall.

The next day in math class I get a note to come to the dean's office. That shaky feeling ripples through me again. Did Mr. Chin decide I was cheating after all? I look at him once while I gather my jacket and books, but his expression says nothing. There's so many lies in my life right now, I can't keep track of which one is worse.

When I get to the office, Mr. Friedlander ushers me in. There's a funny pinch to his face. Beside him is Mrs. Roble, the college counselor. By now my heart is hammering so sharply in my ribs, I'm sure they can hear it.

"Nadira, maybe you can help us out. You know we've always had great faith in your sister. I've never seen a student so gifted, with such poise—" Mrs. Roble hesitates. "I have to tell you. The decision about valedictorian is coming up. Traditionally it's done by grade point average. Since we have several students with about the same average, we've decided to have a vote. Aisha is, of course, a strong candidate. But these last few weeks she's been acting strange. She's skipping classes. I keep asking her for the forms for financial aid. And then I got a call the other day from Barnard—"

At this I perk up. "Yeah?"

"They say she never showed up for her appointment."

I stare at him. "Didn't show up?"

He shakes his head.

"But we were there!"

Mr. Friedlander leans forward. "Nadira, is everything okay with your family? When I called your number, I got a message that your line was disconnected."

"Just some stupid phone company problem," I mumble. I can't meet his eyes.

Mr. Friedlander edges closer. "Nadira, you can tell me. There's so much going on these days. In the news. Have you or Aisha been harassed?"

I almost want to laugh right then. It sounds so simple, so sweet. *Harassed*. I heard about some Pakistani kids walking down Northern Boulevard, and how these cars began swerving toward them and some guys called them dirty Arabs. But that's nothing like the tangle we're in.

"I'll talk to her," I say hoarsely. "I think she's been a little sick, that's all."

As I'm walking away, I hear Mrs. Roble say, "You

know, I've seen this happen before with the Muslim kids. I push those girls—they're so bright. Then one day they come in with a head scarf, and they say their marriage has been arranged and they're not going to college after all." She makes a funny noise through her teeth. "Everything down the tubes, just like that."

My face starts to burn. Then Mr. Friedlander replies, "No, I don't think that's it. That doesn't sound like Aisha."

I find Aisha sitting outside on the bleachers watching the baseball team run laps. It's freezing, but they don't seem to mind. They're dressed in their sweatpants and hooded sweatshirts, and they pound past, breathing out little white puffs of air. Aisha's sitting hunched on the wood planks, her hands stuck in her down jacket.

"How could you go all the way there and not even do the interview?"

She doesn't answer.

"Why are you doing this?"

Still she stays silent. Then she starts to speak, slowly. "I did go. I walked right up to the room. And then I froze. My mind went blank. I got scared. I thought they were going to throw me out." She sucks in her breath. Her cheeks are wet, and she wipes them with her wrist.

"Nadira, I've always been like these guys out here, running. You know me. I'll run in any weather. You give me a test, I'll do ten times better than you expect. I'll do anything." She pushes her hands deeper. "But what if I put myself forward, and then they take everything away?" She shakes her head once more. "And then I realized. I can't do this anymore. It's too hard. Too big. Nothing's working. Not the letters. Nothing. Maybe if I just stop wanting so much, they can't hurt me. I don't want to stand out anymore, Nadira. It hurts too much. I don't want to stand out. Not anymore."

This is the first time I've ever done this, but I put my arms around my sister. She feels as if she's all bones, and she's shaking. I don't know what to say. So we sit like that for a long, long time.

THIRTEEN

I KEEP THINKING ABOUT ABBA AND SWIMMING.

Back in Bangladesh Abba was a great swimmer. When he went to visit his old village, he and the other boys would walk along the banks of the river until they got to the highest point. Abba would clamber up the wide trunk of the banyan tree, swinging himself high into its gnarly branches, and drop right down into the deepest spot in the water.

Everyone would watch him as he stayed below, streaking through the water like a fish. They would count and count and still Abba swam. Sometimes he disappeared from view, and they'd watch the ripples on the surface, wondering how long he could possibly stay down. Finally he'd burst up, a great grin on his face and a squirming crab grasped in his hands.

Strong lungs, they would say of Abba. Strong lungs give him staying power. He's the one who always lasts.

Years later when we moved to Queens, Abba took me to the city pool in Flushing Meadow Park. All his friends gave him a hard time, saying it was shameless what people wore there. I hated that pool—it sits in an old amphitheater, and it's always crowded with kids jumping in from the sides, parents screaming, lifeguards blowing their tinny whistles. While Abba watched, I flapped my arms; I kicked. No matter what I did, I always felt slow and fat and helpless in the water.

On one of his days off Abba took me to the middle of the pool and said it was time I had a proper lesson. He grasped me by the waist and said sternly, "Take a deep breath. Hold it at the back of your throat, like a little soft sack. Then let it out slowly. Slowly."

He placed his palm at the back of my neck and pushed my face down into the bright blue wavelets. Water shot down my throat in a burning spike. I began to sputter and gasp, thrashing my arms at him. Gently, Abba lifted my head up, wiped the salty tears and chlorinated water from my cheeks, then prodded me down again. I squirmed, I cried, but Abba stayed good humored, his hand firm on my neck. Down into the water, again and again. Until I learned how to hold my breath at the back of my throat. How to be slow and patient, let the air out bit by bit in a chain of bubbles. I began to stay down longer, kicking past the tangle of legs and droopy suits. I swam right past them feeling the steady push of my father's hand on my head. By the end of the summer I could swim the whole length of the pool underwater.

When the pool closed in September, Abba cupped his hands around my shoulders and said, "If you know how to breathe, you can get through anything."

That's what I think of now as I get off the bus and walk by the store where Ali-Uncle works. Breathe. Get through this. Find your way to the other side.

No one's home in the apartment. The machine in the kitchen is blinking with a message from Ma. I call her, and her voice sounds funny—both fearful and giddy at once.

"The hearing," she explains. "It's going to happen."

"What will they do?"

"They call it preliminary. To explain the reasons why they're holding your father in there."

"Are you okay?" I ask.

"Yes, Nadira."

She doesn't sound okay, though. Her voice now sounds broken up, like a piece of chalk that's starting to crumble.

"Ma," I say. "Tell me."

"If the hearing goes well, the lawyer says, then maybe your father will be let out. But if it doesn't"—At this she halts. I can hear her breathing on the other end—"If it doesn't, this may also be the beginning of the end. They may deport him right away."

I press my fingers to my temples. I think of Abba in his cell, the soft mound of his stomach rippling, pulling in air, letting it out bit by bit.

What is the right thing to do?

"You can't go to the hearing all by yourself, Ma. Who will translate?"

"Don't worry. They say they have translators here."

After we hang up, I pace the apartment, nerves thrumming. Finally I go into the closet and pull out the folder that has copies of all our hard work. The letters that Aisha and I wrote. The one from Abba's boss and Ali-Uncle. The fax Ma sent to us. Another one she sent a few days ago. Then my eyes light upon Abba's name at the top of Ma's fax. I read it again. A cold sensation tingles through my body to the tips of my fingers. It's like a map that suddenly becomes clear—lines start feeding into each other, connecting the parts. I pull out the new fax, look again. I've got it, I think. I've got a way to get Abba out.

My thoughts are speeding faster, and now one fear trips into another. What if it doesn't work? What if they don't care about my great big discovery? Maybe I have to do something else—something bigger, guaranteed to save Abba. Quickly I dig in my pocket, find the scrap of paper, and dial. The phone picks up after two rings.

"Yo."

"It's me. Nadira."

"Hey!" Tareq sounds genuinely surprised.

"Listen, I was wondering. You know what you said the other day? About helping us out?"

He laughs. "Yeah. Though I have to tell you, it's not cheap."

"I have it. I have money."

There's a pause. "How much?"

I picture Ali-Uncle's slender fingers grazing the pages of the ledger; those tiny, inked figures stacked one after another.

"Three thousand," I tell him.

"Not bad." He tells me to get the money in cash and meet him in Dunkin' Donuts in two hours, and he'll take me where we need to go. I burrow in the closet again. Tucked under an extra pair of jeans I find the money that Ma had given us. There's a hundred dollars left; Auntie wouldn't take much money from us, not even for our food. I peel off most of the bills, pull out a pad of paper, and leave a note. *Don't worry about me,* I scribble. *Everything's going to be all right.*

At the mosque Ali-Uncle lets me go through the file cabinets, pulling papers, lifting up the huge ledger, and making copies on an old Xerox machine that shudders warmly against my legs. When I tell him that I need the three thousand dollars, he gives me an odd look.

"Abba couldn't call you himself, Uncle," I tell him. "So he asked for me to come here. They asked for more money for the bond."

He presses his fingers against his lips. My heart is jabbing fast like a needle against the soft underside of my ribs. It hurts to breathe. Please, I keep thinking. Don't ask questions. Just give it to me. Outside the dark is sweeping down. I have less than an hour to get to the Dunkin' Donuts. I shut my eyes and hear the scrape of Ali-Uncle's chair. Maybe he's calling my aunt and uncle. Then I feel him enter the room; one palm rests warm against my cheek, and the other is folding something into my hands. I open my eyes and see the fat white envelope.

"May Allah go with you," he whispers.

I'm out the door a few minutes later, everything stuffed in my backpack. Outside the air blows warm and mild. I feel strong and solid. Sure. The other day I talked to a girl at college. I've got an envelope of money in my backpack. And now I've got secret business to take care of. I squeeze the strap of my knapsack tighter, adjust its weight on my shoulder. A clump of pigeons is resting on the telephone wire. They flutter up into the sky, the wire bouncing up and down. For the first time I feel like I can run, fast. And I run all the way to the bus.

FOURTEEN

TAREQ'S WAITING IN HIS CAR IN THE PARKING LOT, just like he said. He's slouched down low in the seat, his knee propped against the wheel. His wide face is a mask, his eyes squinty-small. "Get in," he tells me.

When I climb into the passenger seat, he flips open the glove compartment to show his gun inside. His breath is hot and scratchy on my face. "You don't know anything."

"What do you mean?"

"You don't know me, you don't know where I'm taking you. And no names. No shooting your mouth off to your little friends. Get it?"

He pushes the car into gear and squeals out of the lot. He doesn't say anything to me the whole time we're driving. The car weaves in and out of lanes, lights blurring like streaks of wet paint. We're passing Flushing Meadow Park, then we're looping off an exit ramp onto another highway, under a screeching overpass, down some narrow streets. I'm dizzy with all the turns. After a while I sink back into the seat and relax. I like this. It's like going inside the pulsing waves of a TV. The night air is blue, tasting of metal and secrets.

"How does it work, Tareq?" I finally ask.

He frowns. "What did I say, Nadira?"

"Like, hypothetically. That's all."

"This isn't one of those fake social security cards you can buy for not much. This is the real thing. A real social security number, a green card or a U.S. passport. Maybe it's from someone who won a green card in the Diversity Lottery and decided to sell it. Or someone who left for back home, never came back. You can't get busted with this stuff."

I remember our old lawyer, the one who was arrested for something bad.

"—usually it costs a lot more than you've got. But I talked to my contact. He'll make an exception. The papers are for some guy who has amnesty. And the name's pretty close."

We pull up to a brick house with white railing and Christmas lights still strung around the windows. Inside it's just a regular place with plastic slipcovers on the sofa and a dining room where the plates from a meal are still sitting out. A few men are gathered around the table, and I can hear the low warble of a TV on somewhere. We walk in closer, and then I notice it, right next to a dish of rice and meat. A revolver. No one pays attention—it might be a carton of milk for all they care.

"You stay here." Tareq points to the hall.

For a while I wait next to a little table with a bowling trophy and a statue of the Virgin Mary. I can see the men still talking. Tareq's waiting his turn, his hands bunched in front of him. He looks respectful and quiet, different from how he usually is. I can hear voices coming from somewhere. A woman calling. A door slamming. "Mama, I don't want to go to bed!" I hear someone cry, and feet padding upstairs. Then quiet. Tareq is still waiting.

I wander toward the living room, where a boy about my age is sitting cross-legged in front of the TV watching *The Simpsons.* He's a little chubby, and every now and then he lets out a laugh and the folds on his stomach jiggle and shake. Something snags in my throat. I don't want to do this. I don't want to give up Abba's money and do secret business with those men in the other room. I just want to sit with this boy here and laugh at the stupid jokes. I want everything to be the way it was before we went to Canada, when Ma and Abba let me watch TV for an hour every night, and I would rest the back of my head against Abba's legs. Suddenly I can feel it, his words of patience telling me to choose right, even when the storms come.

"I changed my mind," I tell Tareq when he comes looking for me. "I don't want to give them Abba's money."

"What are you talking about?"

"I can't do it." My knees are trembling. I can barely stand. A sour taste bubbles into my mouth. I back out of the hall through the front door.

Once outside I realize I don't even know where I am. I can see Tareq's silhouette looming in the doorway, the blue light of the TV through the lace curtains. Voices shouting. My stomach spasms and I'm doubled over, throwing up into the hedges. Then I run again, blindly, into the dark streets.

FIFTEEN

THAT MONEY IS BURNING A HOLE IN MY KNAPSACK. I'm sure everyone can see it, their eyes scorching X-rays into the white envelope to the crisp bills inside. After I find my way to the subway, there's a lady at the Port Authority who gives me a funny look when I buy my ticket and warns me not to talk to any strangers, and a creepy man who's muttering to himself by the bathroom. Waiting for the bus, I'm sure some policeman is going to nab me by the collar and haul me away. I can see the headlines in the papers. FOURTEEN-YEAR-OLD ILLEGAL ALIEN STOLE ALL HER FAMILY'S MONEY! RUNNING AWAY TO VERMONT! PICKED UP BY SLEAZY GANGSTER IN FRONT OF KRISPY KREME STORE!

On the bus a skinny white guy wearing a Rangers cap keeps giving me funny looks across the aisle. My insides go warm and my stomach gets weak. Maybe he knows. Maybe he's an FBI agent sent by those guys from the other night. Maybe Tareq got some guy to head me off. I try to doze, bunching my coat up to use it as a pillow, but it doesn't help much. The hum and roar of the engine make my stomach bubble sourly again.

We stop about twenty miles north of Boston, where I buy a turkey sandwich and chips. But the turkey slices look slick and shiny, so I throw them away, gnawing on the stale bread instead. Up on the bus station's mounted television, the news is flashing. It makes me nauseous, all those pictures from the war. I don't know what to think, so I stare at my feet until the guy wearing the cap drops himself down next to me, wheezing. Something silver glints in the corner of my eye. I freeze, turn around, and see it's a stick of gum.

"You want some?"

"Thanks." I slide one out and jam it into my mouth. The gum is brittle and tastes of old licorice.

"Where you off to?" he asks. I notice he's missing a tooth.

I hesitate, but he seems harmless. "My mom," I reply.

"Me too. Haven't seen her for five years. She got cancer of the lungs."

I nod. Abba always said you should be careful around strange Americans—they tell you a lot about themselves at first, but they don't mean it.

But this guy wants to talk—whether I do or not. "My mother," he goes on. "She's quite a lady. Married my dad and kicked his butt out when he got mean on her. Never once complained all those years she took care of us."

"How come it's been five years since you've seen her?" I ask. It's the most grown-up question I've ever asked, I realize.

He shrugs. "She lives with my sister, and my mom and I, we don't get along too good."

I don't say anything, but look at his bony profile as he stares out the window. Abba always says that Americans don't know how to be family. It's like this country, he explains; so many long distances between them. But now I'm not so sure he's right. This guy looks pretty sad, and besides, my family doesn't seem to be so close anymore. Taslima and Uncle, they're barely talking these days. And Ma's been gone so long, I can barely imagine her face and smell and hands. Maybe that's what living in America does to you: It spreads you into far distances until you're just little bits rolling apart. It hurts me even to have a thought like that.

The morning sun is out by the time the bus pulls into the Burlington bus station. It's much colder here; the air pinches my toes, and my breath makes little white clouds in the air. I have no idea where I am, but I ask at the counter where the Salvation Army shelter is, and some nice lady tells me which bus to take. She gives me an odd look, but I just turn around, my backpack hiked over my shoulder. Just as I'm leaving the bus station, I see the Rangers guy standing on the corner, grinding a cigarette into the ground. He looks stuck, as if he doesn't know where to go next. I move on without saying good-bye.

The first time I see Ma, she's sitting on her bed, her hands tucked under her thighs. Her head's tipped down, her braid falling straight down her back. Her purple coat is folded over the bed rail. She's sitting so still, I wonder if she's about to kneel on the floor to pray. Then I take a step closer and softly call out.

"Ma? Ma, it's me. Nadira."

Slowly her head lifts. Even from here I can see her face is shiny-wet. She's trembling, hard, and I suddenly realize she wasn't praying, but crying. The next thing I know, she's rushed over to me and flung her arms tight around my neck.

"Oh my God, Nadira. They called me. They said you disappeared."

It's weird having my mother cry in my arms when it should be the other way around. I feel her tremble against me as if she weighs nothing and is made of air. Then she pulls away and looks at me hard. "You naughty girl, how could you scare us like that?" But I can also hear how overjoyed she is to see me because she keeps slapping my arms and patting my stomach. "I should be very angry," she scolds. "What do you think you're doing?"

"I had to run away if I was going to help you with the hearing. Uncle and Auntie would never have let me go. And you wouldn't have either." I don't tell her about going to Tareq—that would really upset her.

She smiles. "That's true." She stands and pats me

on the arm. "Come, then, since you're here. I'll take you out for lunch."

It turns out that Ma, in her own way, has made a lot of friends up here. There's the woman guard downstairs, Doris, who didn't give me a hard time about getting upstairs and has taken a fancy to Ma, whom she calls the Purple Lady With the Sing-Song Voice. And then there's the cafeteria next door where every day Ma eats all her meals. The women there have grown fond of her, charging her for only half the dishes she orders. They ask about how Abba is doing and how the case is going, and they know all about Aisha and how she may be valedictorian.

"This is my younger daughter," she says proudly, guiding me past the steam table. The women, all of whom have round faces and their hair bound into nets, smile and wave their gloved hands. "Your mother's the best," one lady tells me. "I never seen a lady so brave. Every day she sits outside that courthouse doing what she has to do."

I can't believe it. Back in New York, Ma barely ever went out of the house unless she was accompanied by us. Unlike Auntie she didn't work at a store, and she rarely spoke English, though I know she was practicing all that time. I would come home and find her sitting at the table imitating the words from her cooking shows. Abba used to tease her that the only job she could ever get in America was as a cook because she knew all the English words about food, but she couldn't get on a bus by herself to save her life.

Not this Ma. After we eat, we head back to the shelter where she changes into a fresh set of clothes—western clothes, to my surprise: a dark blue skirt and a blue shirt not much different from what Aisha wore that day for Mr. Rashid. She puts on her purple coat and smoothes her hair, and then she hooks her hand through my arm. We go downstairs and she leads me to the bus stop. She does all this like she's been doing it for years. I keep waiting for her to pull back or to ask me to translate something.

The bus arrives. She puts the money in and sits up straight on the seat the whole way. When we enter the big gray building, she doesn't even flinch when the guards run their electronic wands up and down her sides, under her legs, across her chest. I'm sure any minute she's going to start crying in shame. But she doesn't. Her face is set, and she waits for me on the other side while the guards make me take off my sneakers. "Follow me," she instructs after they finish and leads me upstairs.

I keep expecting to enter some kind of huge courtroom, just like on TV. I have my papers in my backpack, and I want to run down the aisle like I'm in some movie scene and stop in front of the defense table and wave my arms. "Evidence!" I'd cry. "I've got all the evidence!" I wish there were a jury lined against one wall and a black-robed judge towering from his seat, banging a polished gavel.

Instead we're ushered into a small room that smells of old cigarettes. There's a long table in the middle strewn with papers and empty Styrofoam cups.

Our lawyer—the court appointed one—sits beside us holding a stack of folders. He looks tired; purplish circles ring his eyes. When he starts to talk, his voice also sounds tired, as if he's been through this too many times.

"We only have a few minutes, Mrs. Hossein, before the judge and other authorities will be here."

"What will happen?" asks Ma.

"From what I can tell, this is just a preliminary hearing. It's a process by which you are given some idea for the reasons behind your husband's detainment."

I sit up. "But please, sir, if I may, there's something—"

His eyes flicker impatiently. "This is not time for any special pleas. Our aim is to argue as forcefully as possible that your husband is not a security risk, so there are no grounds for his detainment."

"I know that, sir! That's exactly it. I have—"

We're interrupted by the judge walking in along with a lady who takes her place at a funny machine—almost like a typewriter but smaller, like a shoebox with tiny buttons. Two other men join them, but it's all happening so fast I can't figure out who is who.

Then the door opens and in walks Abba.

I had forgotten I would see my father. All along he's been no more than a voice in my head, a shape in the walls, urging me to be patient. I picture him sometimes, standing over a sink running a washcloth over his arms, slow and careful, never rushing. Other times he's sitting on a stool in the kitchen with newspapers at his feet, instructing Ma how to cut the back of his hair. Most often I see him sitting very still, breathing slowly as he told me to do.

But the man who walks in is not the Abba I know. Tufts of scraggly black hair spring from his cheeks. And his clothes! Abba, who is always so particular—sometimes he chides Ma if she doesn't crease his shirt just so—has on the same shirt he wore the last day I saw him. Ragged yellow stains show under his arms, and there's a little tear at the elbow. His pants sag off his hips. I cannot believe this is the same Abba who sometimes took more than an hour to bathe, carefully oiling his hair and clipping his toenails.

"Nadira," he whispers. "You're here." He drops down in a chair opposite us. He's got this goofy smile on his face, sort of sloppy and tilted. One of his teeth bites on his lower lip, which makes him look silly.

Abba, I want to say. Please sit up straight.

When the hearing begins, I can't concentrate. Voices float toward me in snatches as if underwater.

"You realize we have grounds for deportation right now. Your client has several violations on his visa. He changed residence three times without informing the INS."

"But these are minor infractions! We've already established that his original lawyer didn't file properly."

"This is not just about something minor," the judge continues. "Mr. Hossein is being held in conjunction with an investigation of religious organizations that may be sponsoring illegal activities. At this point all I can do is enter into the file any information regarding his relationship to this fund. If you have any, that is."

The lawyer riffles through the folder. "I have none."

"All right, then." The judge starts to scribble something on a piece of paper. He is an older man, round faced like those women in the cafeteria. A pair of rimless glasses perch on his nose, giving him a vague look. He doesn't look mean or bad; he just looks tired, like everyone else.

I press my palms on the table and stand. "May I speak?"

The lawyer glances at me, annoyed. I don't care—I'm digging into my knapsack and pulling out our folder. Inside I find the letter that Ali-Uncle wrote and my Xeroxes, which I pass around.

At first I can't get the words out—it's like pushing against a wall of water. I want to tell them more than just that I have proof that Abba was just putting money away for our tuition. I want to tell them that Abba's favorite show is *The Simpsons* and that he loves Tagore. I want to say that sometimes you can't know who a person is. Sometimes they don't know who they are either. They can appear to be one thing—like me, fat and slow and lazy—but you can look at them another way too— and see something else.

I have lungs, I want to tell them. I have lungs that can hold so much air, and I know how to let it go, bit by bit, so I can stand it even when Abba is sitting here, crushed and weak, looking like a father I never knew. But I know. I also know who I am and they must look at our papers and see who we are too.

Instead, I hold my breath and say, "You've got the wrong person."

"What?"

I push all the papers toward them and start pointing. "See. That one is spelled with an *e*. And look at my father's papers, how he spells his name with an *a*." I slide out the Xerox. "And see here. There's another guy with the same name who spells it with an *e*, and he also gave to the fund. He lives in Florida now—that's where he sends his money from. But he's 'Hossein' with an *e*. Not my father."

It happens all the time, I think. Like sometimes they write *Nadeera* for *Nadira*. Or I've seen *Nadra*, too. *Ayesha* for *Aisha*. We don't keep track of half the spellings, and I remember one time the immigration lawyer yelled at us because we'd filed papers with three different names by mistake.

The judge snaps his folder shut and holds up his palm. "Wait a minute. I can countenance some confusion here—Vermont, New York, different jurisdictions. But you don't even have the *name* right?"

One of the agents who is squinting at my papers coughs. "It appears not, sir."

"And there's something else," I put in. "About the fund."

My hands are trembling as I fish out the envelope

from my backpack and shake out the money—stacks of bills bound with a rubber band. "That's my dad's money," I tell them. I slide Ali-Uncle's letter across the table too. "See what this says? It wasn't some contribution. It's how Abba saved his money. For us."

Everyone stares at all that money lying in a pile on the table. The lady punching the funny machine has a little smile on her face.

"This is rather unusual," the judge says. He seems afraid to lift up the letter, but he puts on his glasses and reads. Then he turns to Abba. "Is this true, what this letter says, that your deposits with this account were to pay for your children's tuition?"

Abba perks up. "Yes, yes! My daughter, she is A plus student. And my other daughter . . ." Here he trails off. He seems to want to smile, but is afraid, so instead he licks his cracked lips. "You see my brilliant girl here."

Even the agents can't resist making small, dry smiles. One of them leans forward and examines the letter from Ali-Uncle. He whispers to the other agent, and they talk in low voices for a few minutes.

The judge is getting impatient. "Can we please be filled in, gentlemen?"

"You say your contributions were under the name Hossain spelled with an *a*?

Abba nods vigorously.

"And not Hossein spelled with an *e*?"

"No."

The judge throws his pen down. His glasses glitter

on the edge of his nose. "You folks make a simple mistake and this—" He turns to me, grinning. "What grade are you in, dear?"

"Ninth," I answer.

"This ninth grader can straighten it out in five minutes! Does anyone do their homework here?" Everyone stares at their feet, embarrassed. The judge turns to us. "Mr. and Mrs. Hossain, there does appear to be a mistake in identification." He pauses and looks over at Abba. "I apologize, Mr. Hossain. You see how it is here. We're coordinating with so many agencies, and there's been so many cases—we're overwhelmed."

Abba barely gives a nod.

"The situation here is very serious. A name mix-up can't clear up all the other discrepancies. You are still in violation of your visa and could face deportation proceedings."

Ma grabs my hand. The judge is scribbling something down. "However it's clear you've been given quite the runaround these past few years. And in light of your unnecessary and prolonged detainment, I've suggested that Immigration hear your appeal for residency one more time."

"Appeal?" Even Abba lifts up his face.

"I have no control over their decision. But I will forward all your papers for another review." He glances, just once, at me, and I swear there's a slight smile twitching at his lips. I start to flush.

Ma has been watching the judge's lips move, but her

eyes are blank. "My husband can go now?" she stammers.

"Yes," the judge replies. He points to the money stacks on the table. "And please. Put that away in a safe place."

Grinning, I stuff the stacks back in the envelope.

The policemen walk us to some office where Abba has to be fingerprinted and photographed again, and he signs some papers. The lawyer explains that we'll be hearing from Immigration in the next few weeks. I'm almost disappointed because he makes it sound as if it's all just procedure. I didn't save Abba. Or maybe I did, in a small way. I made them stop and see me—see *us*. Take a second look. Ma sat beside me in her proud purple coat, and I spoke.

All I keep thinking is I can't wait to tell Aisha.

SIXTEEN

YOU HAVE A FAMILY, AND YOU GO AROUND THINKING it's always one way. Ever since I could remember, Aisha was the star we pinned our future on. It's as if Ma and Abba were still in Bangladesh riding in a flat bottomed boat in the night, and Aisha was the magic girl who lived above the dark tree branches and lit the way, leading us down the complicated bends. Now all the stars are no more than rubber stickers pasted on a ceiling; they've come unfastened and they're whirling around one another, not sure which will settle where.

But sometimes there's someone else, especially when the sky goes dark: the person guiding slowly from behind. That's who I've become in my family. The whole way back on the bus Ma keeps giving me these tight squeezes on my arm as if I'm suddenly real to her. And Abba touches my hair and keeps repeating, "You did a good thing. A very good thing, Nadira. You used your head in a right way."

And I keep looking at my reflection in the bus window, and I know it's true.

When we return, Auntie cooks for hours—all through the evening and the next day too—and then they invite everyone over to celebrate Abba's return. We deflate the air mattress where Aisha and I now sleep and push the sofa back against the wall. All day long people come back to welcome Abba. He pats me on the head and doesn't let me go into the kitchen with the women, but makes sure I sit right next to him. I'm embarrassed, but I like this, being the special one.

Abba tells the same story over and over—the long days in his jail cell, the letters we sent, and the way I showed up like a hero-lawyer in a TV show, showed them all that money, made the judge look again. Everyone ripples with laughter, shakes their heads. Taslima punches me in the arm. "A regular episode of *Law and Order*," she teases. Even Ali-Uncle comes by and first scolds me for lying to him, and then praises me for knowing how to find the truth. We stay up late drinking tea and stuffing ourselves with fish and lamb and rice. It's like holding a bubble aloft in the air; everyone is so light and happy, full of jokes. And it is only after the last paper plates are folded into the trash, the pots scrubbed and turned over to dry on towels, and the apartment falls quiet again that I realize none of this can last.

For the next few days we try to get back to normal. All of us squeeze into the apartment, though it isn't easy.

Abba and Ma take Taslima's room, and we girls sleep in the living room. Abba is nervous about having the money around, so we go into Flushing and open a real bank account and deposit it there. But I can feel the tension in the air: Auntie and Uncle whispering fiercely in the dark after everyone has gone to sleep; Taslima sneaking off when no one is looking.

On Sunday everyone relaxes and watches cricket on the satellite TV. After lunch Ma and I keep Abba company as he takes a slow walk around the neighborhood while Auntie and Uncle visit friends and Aisha and Taslima stay home. At least that's what we thought.

We return to find the apartment in an uproar. Suitcases are flung open on the floor, and Auntie's tossing socks and clothes inside, weeping. Uncle's rolling up the rug. All the cupboards are opened, half-empty of dishes and cans. Aisha's huddled on the sofa, her knees drawn to her chest.

"What's going on here?" Ma asks, looking puzzled at the floor.

"Ask your precious daughter," Uncle mutters.

"Aisha?" Ma's purple coat spreads around her as she kneels in front of my sister. "What happened?"

Aisha says nothing.

"I'll tell you then! Your A plus student hasn't gone to school for days! She hasn't done anything! Turns out the only thing she has done is help my miserable daughter leave!"

"Leave?"

"She's gone to live with that boyfriend of hers! When everyone was out, Aisha helped her pack, and they took everything over there. She says she'll marry him to spite us."

"But why?"

"Because I've decided we should go back to Bangladesh." He kicks the rug. "Better I am poor in a country where I can feel at home. Where I am wanted, than to live like this."

"But what about Canada?" Abba asks. "You can come with us."

Uncle shakes his head. "Enough. I cannot beg anymore."

Auntie gets up from the table and starts pulling down mittens, hats, and gloves from a basket in the closet. "I'll leave this all for you," she says to Ma. "If you go to Canada, you'll be warm."

Ma isn't listening, though. She's peering at Aisha, whom she seems not to recognize. "What's this I hear? No school?"

Aisha doesn't answer.

"What about graduation? The interview, all that?"

Without replying Aisha retreats into Taslima's bedroom. Abba and Ma stand there frozen, their faces drawn and tired. I bang on the door. There's no answer. I push open the door and see Aisha sitting at the end of the room on the edge of the bed, her hands folded in her lap. I can't see her very well because the lights are dimmed.

"Aisha," I whisper.

She doesn't answer, so I move nearer. Now I can see her hair has been pulled into a lumpy braid.

"Aisha, what's going on? How can you let everything go like that?"

She shakes her head. "I can't. I'm ashamed."

"What do you mean?"

"Mr. Friedlander, he kept sending me notes. But I couldn't even go to his office. I couldn't do anything. All I want to do is sit here in the dark and not move."

"We can go to Mr. Friedlander. We can tell him what happened. He'll understand. I bet they'll make you valedictorian for sure."

She rubs her fists on her knees. "All of that seems so far away now. It doesn't matter."

Later that night Aisha and I lie on either end of the sofa bed and turn out the lamp. The comforter smells like Taslima, and I feel a little sad. I kind of miss her, even though it was always too noisy when she was around. This is what I was afraid of. Now it's all chaos and choppy water around us again—shoes flying into suitcases, and everyone quarreling at once. Aisha and I just lie there. I can feel her breathing beside me. When I fall asleep, I know she's still awake, staring into the dark.

Four days later Auntie and Uncle are gone, flown in a Biman plane to Dhaka. Uncle's thick black waiter shoes sit in the bare closet while Auntie's chili plants wilt in their pots. The apartment feels too large, too echoey, for the four of us.

Ma is most definitely not the same. She insists on wearing that purple coat everywhere, all the time, even though it's warm out. And she doesn't walk behind Abba as in the old days, but gently leads him along while he gets his strength back. Now she settles him down on the sofa with a small blanket across his knees. She treats him like an elder brother whose brain is a little addled. Now that all the celebrating is done, Abba sits still and quiet, all squinty frowns and disheveled clothes. He lost weight during the months he was in detainment; the little mound of his belly no longer slopes over his belt, and his elbows stick out in flinty triangles.

Ever since she got back, Ma likes to bustle around with all kinds of pronouncements. "If we go to Canada, I want to make sure that Nadira takes up some kind of sport. All this sitting around isn't good for her." Or "If we stay in New York, I want yellow curtains. Not those dark blue ones that had me so sad all the time." She's cheerful and optimistic, whereas Abba is drawn and sad.

Mr. Rashid is hoping the appeal will come through. Otherwise we'll try again for Canada. Abba doesn't believe we'll get asylum there, either. He doesn't believe there's a future there for him. There's only his hands spread across his knees, the curtain shifting in the window.

Even though Abba and Aisha are proud of what I did,

they can't seem to be happy. They've both withdrawn into the same dark, brooding room. No light ever seems to get in. I think it's because the two of them hoped so hard; when things started going wrong for us they broke inside.

Meanwhile the college envelopes, they've started coming. Stony Brook. Binghamton. Hunter. Bryn Mawr. They sit, fat and unopened, on the dining room table until Aisha stacks them together. "Open them!" I prod her, but she shakes her head.

"Why should I? Look at their tuition. We can't pay that."

"There's got to be a way, Aisha."

"What way?" she asks softly and slides the envelopes into her dresser drawer.

Today the mail is very late. It's almost supper time when I hear the mailman with his jangling keys slam the thin metal mailbox doors in the downstairs lobby. Ma has run to the butcher to buy some end-of-the-day meat. Downstairs I see we've received another fat envelope. Only this one isn't from a college. Stamped in the left-hand corner is a U.S. Government seal. I pick it up, weigh it in my hands. I bring the envelope to Abba, who's sitting on a chair by the window with a blanket across his knees, and I leave it on his lap. Aisha, washing dishes, stops to watch. He stares at the envelope a few seconds, then slowly, slowly opens it up. I can see, the way his eyes are moving that he's having trouble with the English. So I take it from his trembling fingers and read aloud.

"Scheduled court appearance: June 12. Final appeal on residency status."

Aisha flings down her dish towel, goes into the bedroom, and brings out her stack of envelopes to the dining table. She starts ripping them in half, one by one.

"What are you doing?" I ask.

"Come on, Nadira. This is just a formality. We have to leave."

"No, the judge, he said we'd have an appeal."

"Oh please." She jerks her hand away. "You are such a baby. Do you really believe a little fourteen-year-old can make the United States government change its mind?" She tears another envelope in two and pushes chunks of ripped-up paper into a mound in the center of the table.

I have to leave. I can't stay in here anymore, so I run downstairs. Outside, waves of silver heat ripple off the pavement. I don't care. I run all the way to Ali-Uncle's store, my breaths short and sharp in my lungs. The windows are pitch dark, and the metal grate is pulled shut; a padlock dangles off one side. I cup my hands and peer inside. The racks are empty of magazines; I can see the cash register is unplugged.

"Gone," says a voice behind me.

Mr. Kim, the dry cleaner, is standing on the pavement. "One day he just gone." He snaps his fingers.

"Who?"

"Owner. And man who work for him?"

"Ali-Uncle?"

"Yeah, that guy. Just like that. He come in and give me box of Coca-Cola and leave the key for landlord. Then he go."

"Did he say where?"

Mr. Kim shakes his head. "No say. He look different. No beard. Hair short. Not look good." He shrugs. "Very strange. But bad things maybe happen to him."

He points to his store, where there are Coke cans stacked in the front. "You want a soda, maybe?"

I take a can and trudge down the street to the playground. When we first moved to Queens, the only time we were allowed out other than for school was for one hour in the afternoons when Ma would take us here. Aisha would clamber onto the monkey bars, and I would push on the swings. Ma was so afraid then; she feared any minute Aisha would crack her skull on the pavement, or someone would snatch us away. There were too many dangers, she complained in the beginning, too much that could go wrong here.

Swinging up on the bars, I climb all the way to the top and watch the people walk home, all of them limp from the heat, the men with their shirts unbuttoned, the women holding sacks of groceries, their legs bare. A few lights are blinking on in windows, making a checkerboard of brightness and shadow in the buildings. All those people, I think. Maybe if we knocked on their doors and just asked them to sponsor us, they would do it. It would be the opposite of those milk carton ads—instead of missing children, we would be found children. A found family. That's all it would take. One door, opening.

"Hey." I swivel around. To my surprise Aisha is standing below me, shading her eyes with her palm.

"Sorry for before."

"How'd you find me?"

"Mr. Kim told me where you went."

She hesitates, then pulls herself up on the monkey bars. "I can't believe Ali's gone," she whispers. "Abba's right. We don't have a future here. That's why I tore up those letters. I couldn't be valedictorian anyway."

"Aisha, I hate to say it, but it's your own fault, messing up so much."

"Forget it." She reaches for the can and takes a gulp. "It's all the same. How could I get up there in public and act like I'm some representative of the class? I can't even go to college like the rest of them. I don't even know where I'm going to live. That's not right. That's not who the valedictorian is."

We sit for a few minutes balanced on the monkey bars. I remember how Ali-Uncle used to sing songs or recite poetry while we stacked newspapers. Sometimes I thought they were stupid or corny, about places in Bengal that I don't even remember. But now I can feel him pressing his fingers lightly into my neck, telling me to look up.

Above, the sky looks gray and soupy, like water before a storm. A few pale, weak stars glimmer through. I can feel all of our elders breathing down on us. Ali-Uncle. Naseem-Uncle. I shut my eyes, imagine the dappled swimming pool shot through with sunlight. It's not just about breathing. It's about making yourself clear as water, honest and calm.

"Aisha," I say. "I want to tell you about what happened in Vermont. In front of the judge and everything."

Her eyes grow small. "So?"

"It wasn't just that I showed them their mistake. It was more than that. I let them see us. And maybe that's not the only reason Abba was released. But it made a difference. I know it did."

She laughs, tipping the can against her teeth, her voice sounding hollow and tinny. "Do you really believe that?"

"Yes."

She snorts.

"I always thought you were the brave one. But now I think you're a coward, Aisha." I see her stiffen a little, but still I press on. "You gave up because everything stopped being easy. Just because you couldn't conquer this thing like you always did. I think, Aisha, that you're always thinking about doing or saying the right thing. Wearing the right clothes. Blending in. But sometimes . . . sometimes you have to tell them who you are. What you really think. You have to make them *see* us."

She doesn't say anything at first. "And how do we do that?" she asks.

"You and me, we're going to talk to Mr. Friedlander."

She blanches. "No."

"We're going to tell him everything. The whole truth. And we're going to say it's got to be you up there at graduation."

"But Abba and Ma will never let us—"

"Sometimes we have to do the right thing. In our own way."

I swing down, the soles of my feet stinging as I hit the ground. When I turn around, I see Aisha's still up there, looking pale and uncertain. She was never very good at sports, and Abba used to make fun of her for inheriting his pigeon-toed walk. Now she slowly raises herself on the monkey bars. Her sandals don't give her much traction. She's tipping back and forth, legs trembling, one hand gripping the can.

"Come on!" I call. "It's not that far!" I hold out both hands. The hot air wavers between us. Then Aisha lets her arms float to her sides and she jumps toward me.

SEVENTEEN

AISHA'S SHAKING EVEN AS SHE GETS UP FROM HER seat in the first row. I know because Aisha wouldn't give her speech unless I sat with the graduates. This is yours too, she said. So here I am, sweating in the tweed blazer Ma made me wear, sitting next to kids three years older than me. Risa's nearby too, her cap tilted on her frizzy hair. She looks relieved that Aisha got her chance. The air-conditioning is broken in the auditorium, and everywhere little programs are flapping like dozens of impatient white birds.

Somewhere behind me is Abba, dressed up in a suit that's too big for him, and Ma, and next to them, Taslima, who wears a sliver of gold on her finger now. She's married—at City Hall she said. One day she'll exist on paper in this country. She can sit on buses and take classes and get a job and never again feel that churning in her stomach if someone asks for ID. I feel a little burn of envy, and then it's gone, vanished into the blue sky outside.

Not far from them I can just make out Cassie David, this reporter and a friend of Mr. Friedlander's. He called her right after we told him what was going on, and then she met us a few days ago and wrote a story about an illegal family: one daughter who was a high school valedictorian, and another who exposed a case of mistaken identity to the federal government. PRIZE STUDENT FACES DEPORTATION. Under the headline it read: POINTS OUT FLAWS IN REGISTRATION PROGRAM. REPRIEVE CONSIDERED.

Aisha's stepping onto the stage, and as she lifts the bottom of her gown, I can see the high heels Ma let her buy. They had a real fight about it too, in the Parade Shoes store, but finally Ma relented and there they are: bright, shiny red satin heels with skinny straps. She leans against the podium and adjusts her cap. Her curly waves bounce just a little. She taps the microphone and a thudding noise hammers from the speakers. Flustered, she pulls back.

Do it, I signal. *Do it.*

She runs her tongue over her teeth. The room has grown still; everyone has stopped flapping their programs. I can see Mr. Friedlander on the stage shifting uncomfortably in his folding chair.

And then she says them: the words that have gathered like thunder in our throats. The words that make me afraid to move in my own skin.

"My name is Aisha Hossain. And I am an illegal alien."

Behind me I hear hundreds of gasps. I don't move, but I can see them: the girls and boys we pass in the halls every day; the mothers in their nice summer dresses and the fathers tapping the rolled up program on their knees; the little brothers and sisters squirming in their seats.

"I am an illegal alien," Aisha repeats, harder, faster now. She has both hands on the side of the podium, and she's leaning into it like it's an animal she needs to ride.

"My family came here eight years ago on a tourist visa and stayed. My father worked every job he could. We paid a lawyer to make us legal, but then he disappeared. We hired another lawyer to do the same thing, but it didn't work.

"In those days they didn't enforce the laws. We were the people you don't always see, flashing our polite smiles, trimming hedges, parking your cars in lots, doing the night shift. You needed us and we needed you."

She swallows some water. "And then one day two planes came and smashed into two towers. A war started. Overnight, we, the invisible people, became visible. We became dangerous. We became terrorists, people with bombs in our luggage, poison in our homes.

"My father—" Here she pauses. When she starts again, the words are wobbling a little out of her mouth. "My father just wanted to do the right thing. For us. He drove us to Canada because he thought that was for the best. But we couldn't get in, so the authorities took him away. For many weeks. They said he gave money to a suspicious organization. It wasn't true. And none of those things tell you who he is or who we are.

"I got scared for him. I got scared for me, too. I got scared that they would take me away in the middle of the night.

"I tell none of this to make you pity me. I understand there are bad people in the world. But you have to understand what happened to my father. Because for all those years, my Abba—all of us—believed. They let us in, and they let us believe that we belonged. That we could hope for a future here. That one day I could go to college and carry on. And then they took that hope away. They broke my father's heart. And they broke mine, too."

She pauses. "All I ask of you is to see me for who I am. Aisha. I spell my name not with a *y* or an *e*, but with an *i*. See me. I live with you. I live near you. I go to your school; I eat in your cafeteria; I take the same classes. Now I am your valedictorian. I want what you want. I want a future."

She tucks her head down, and I can see she's really crying now; her small shoulders tremble. My own tears trickle, salty and hot, into my mouth. "Thank you," she whispers.

An instant later she's gone from the stage.

EIGHTEEN

LAST NIGHT I DREAMED WE WERE SWIMMING INSIDE a map. On one side the river flowed to the border of Canada, a skinny blue-green line wriggling into the distance. On the other side the courthouse floated, an underwater dungeon of hazy stone glinting with jeweled windows. We shut our eyes, not sure which way to go. We dove inside and the land dissolved, silt melting into sea. We pushed ahead, heads bowed, blindly groping forward.

"Shahid! Nadira! Hurry! *Cholo!*"

It's Ma standing in the middle of the living room, her hands on her hips. I pull myself up, dazed at the rumpled covers around me. Warm buttery light is pouring through the windows. The sky is already white from the sun. It's going to be another hot day.

As I get dressed, I can hear my mother scolding. "Shahid, hurry now, you don't want to be late." Or "No, not those socks, they don't match the pants." Abba's wearing the same suit he wore to Aisha's graduation two days ago, only this time Ma's ironed it extra sharp with a crisp crease running down the trouser legs. "I don't want you looking like some street bum," she remarks as she hands him the trousers carefully folded over her arm.

Aisha's sitting at the table. She looks very calm with her ankles pressed together, her hands folded on her lap. Her thick hair has been oiled and clamped down with big plastic barrettes, making her look a little funny. She grins at me when she sees I've got my graduation clothes on too, only there's a small, ragged orange stain on my shirt pocket. That's from when we went to eat at a restaurant after, and I spilled some tandoori sauce on me.

The funny thing is, even though Ma's the one that's been hurrying us all morning, it's she who's late. We sit there, itchy in our good clothes, waiting while she's in the bathroom finishing up. "Ma!" Aisha calls. "Come on already!"

When Ma comes out, we're all stunned. She looks beautiful, if a little strange. No *shalwar kameez* with embroidered cuffs at the ankle; no billowy chiffon *dupatta*. She's wearing a western-style dress—it's a blue and red pattern with a thin yellow belt that cinches tight at her waist. And her hair has been swept up into a gleaming black topknot. She looks like an airline stewardess nervously brushing the table of crumbs, checking and rechecking that the stove is turned off.

"It's time," she whispers and turns off the light before shutting the door.

Aisha is driving today, her hands loose on the wheel, her hair lifting lightly in the breeze. Ma and I sit in the back, and Abba tries not to comment on her driving. Ma keeps patting her big floppy bag. Inside is everything we need, depending on what happens today. We have our folder with all the papers for our appeal. And a scrap of paper with an address of a friend of a cousin, directions to Toronto, folders for university for Aisha.

Since we're early, we stop for lunch at a McDonald's, sitting in a plastic booth and watching the cars skim by.

"Nadira, how can you even eat that junk?" Aisha is pointing to my extra-large portion of french fries. "Don't you know there's some kids who are actually suing McDonald's for their obesity?"

"It tastes good," I answer, folding a fry into my mouth. It goes down salty in my throat. I eat a few more, push the container away, and suck down my Coke, the ice rattling in my paper cup. "If we go to Canada," I suddenly declare, "I'm not going to eat any McDonald's. I'll only eat Canadian food."

Aisha giggles. "What's that?"

"I don't know." I try to figure out what that could be. At school, before we left, I pulled out a book about Canada but didn't learn much. They speak French in one place, I learned, and they get off the day after Christmas, for a holiday called Boxing Day.

"If we even get to Canada," Abba puts in. "I don't know why you all talk about this as if it's so certain."

It's rare that Abba says much these days. I think it's gnawing at him, all those weeks in detainment. The day after we received our notice of an appeal, he put on his best waiter's pants and white shirt and went to see Mr. Rashid. He came back later that afternoon, his skin a grayish color, his eyes downcast. Mr. Rashid said he couldn't tell what would happen. Either we'd get our residency or we'd be deported in thirty days. As if bracing for the worst, this time Abba called our relatives and spoke softly to them on the phone. He took a tour of the neighborhood, wishing Mr. Kim and the other shopkeepers a full and happy life. For days he moved through the house as if he were made of glass; one bump, one bad word, and I feared he might shatter.

Ma squints up at the sky. "We better go," she declares, slapping her palms on her dress. She crushes the empty bags and carries the tray over to the garbage. When she returns, she notices Abba, still sitting on the bench, his large hands spread across his knees. He's gazing down at the floor between his feet. He looks like he never wants to leave.

"Come now," she whispers in his ear, and gently lifts him up toward the car.

It's afternoon when we pull into the lot next to the courthouse. An American flag flaps on a huge pole, and yellow ribbons are tied to the pillars of the entrance. Long shadows slant like thin blades through the wire mesh fence. Security guards are everywhere, patrolling the parked cars, checking the people as they trickle into the different entrances. My stomach starts to jump like there's a tiny Super Ball bouncing inside. I'm glad I didn't eat the rest of my fries—I'd probably throw up right now, on the seats, and embarrass myself.

A guard heads over to our car and asks for our IDs. Abba, who's sitting in the passenger seat this time, leans to the left, clutching our computer printout. I can see his hand is shaking. "Please, sir," he says. "We have a very important hearing here today."

The man scans the paper, checks our worn Bangladeshi passports, and hands them back to him. Then the man steps back and waves us toward the parking lot. Just like that. Like it's nothing.

Slowly, Aisha noses the car into the lot. We sit there a few moments listening to the engine tick. I keep trying to remember what Abba said about his meeting with Mr. Rashid. *There are no guarantees. This is the last chance. We've run out of options.* A man hurries past us, a bulging folder under his arm, his tie flying to the side. Suddenly it all seems impossible. All those years of forms and phone calls and faxes and waiting; all those other people who must be inside sitting tiredly on benches with their papers and folders. The courthouse suddenly seems a maze of stone, its corridors squeezed shut of light and hope.

We get out dizzy, wobbly kneed. Ma palms her hair

down over and over. The cement lot is huge as an ocean glittering in the sun, impossible to cross. I can barely feel my legs, they're so numb.

Inside the courtroom I see the reporter, Cassie David, waiting on a bench with a narrow notebook propped on her knees. We don't even smile at her—Mr. Rashid told us not to. Now we sit down beside him, and I notice he's dressed up extra smart in a crisp white shirt and black suit, and he keeps touching his hair, which is smoothed back with shiny oil.

The judge is a woman, young, the robe falling a little too full on her shoulders. She frowns, looks at the files, and asks some questions. "You are aware, Mr. Hossain, that, no matter what the extenuating circumstances, you are in violation of your visa and have put your entire family in jeopardy?"

Abba swallows and nods.

"And that it is the responsibility of the applicant to ensure that all materials are filed properly?"

Again Abba nods.

Her mouth twitches. She gazes at the four of us gathered in a tight arc—at our small, worried faces.

"Well. This is an unusual case. I grant you permission to file a new application for residency. Your papers will be accepted and processed. Correctly this time." She pauses with the faintest hint of a smile and looks sharply at Mr. Rashid. "And make sure your lawyer does his job." She pushes the folder away. "Next!"

When the gavel cracks, wood on wood, the air seems

to explode with light. Abba turns around and I see he is crying silent tears. But he says nothing. Not to Mr. Rashid, who is congratulating him, or the reporter, who is pushing toward us, notebook in hand, or the judge. He watches as Aisha grabs Ma's elbow. Ma links her arm into mine and leans her weight into me, just a little.

Then Abba looks at us all. "Ready to go home?"

Together we shut our eyes, dip our heads, and start to leave the room. I can feel it, the water pressing all around us, pulsing from below. Abba's fingers reach for mine.

And we do as he taught us. We hold our breaths, then let them out, bit by bit.

We push forward, into the unknown. *Go.*

ENDNOTE

In the wake of the September 11 terrorist attacks, the U.S. government began a crackdown on illegal immigrants and an investigation of Muslim communities. All Muslim men over the age of eighteen from certain countries were required to register. If they were found to be residing illegally, or if they had any minor infractions on their visas, they were jailed, detained, or deported. Though the government eventually ended the registration program, under the newly enacted Patriot Act the FBI was given the power to raid businesses and homes and detain immigrants for questioning. Many of these men remained in jails for months on end without legal representation or being formally charged. Some spoke of being abused. Families were not allowed to visit them, and their hearings were closed to the public.

During this period hundreds of immigrants, not sure what would happen to them, fled to the

Canadian border, though many were turned back only to be arrested by U.S. immigration authorities. Many of these people were immigrants who had lived for years in the U.S., and their children had been raised as Americans.

Although this is a work of fiction, these are the events that inspired this book.